"Maybe I Just Don't Like You."

She hoped he didn't hear the quiver in her voice, or feel her hands trembling.

He shook his head. "Nah, that can't be it. I mean, look at me. I'm handsome and rich."

"And modest."

He grinned. "Exactly. What's not to like?"

She had the feeling he wasn't nearly as arrogant and shallow as he wanted her to believe, that maybe it was some sort of…defense mechanism. And boy did she know about those.

"Admit it," he said. "You like me."

"You're my boss," she said, but it came out all soft and breathy.

His eyes locked on hers. "Not after we walked out of the building."

* * *

Dear Reader,

Welcome to the fourth and final installment of my Black Gold Billionaires series! I can hardly believe it's over already. In my eight years as a published author I've never had so much fun writing a series. These guys—and gals—have really challenged me, and I just loved telling their individual stories. And I must admit that, while I find Adam, Emilio and Nathan exceptional in their own ways, Jordan holds a special place in my heart. He's a little arrogant, but he doesn't take himself too seriously and he has a wicked sense of humor. He also manages to draw Plain Jane Monroe out of her shell. I think you'll enjoy their love story, and also find a few interesting surprises along the way.

As I write this, I'm already plotting out my next series, which might take place in Chicago, and may involve babies. But you'll just have to wait and see....

Best,

Michelle

MICHELLE CELMER

MUCH MORE THAN A MISTRESS

Harlequin®

Desire

Recycling programs
for this product may
not exist in your area.

ISBN-13: 978-0-373-73124-4

MUCH MORE THAN A MISTRESS

Copyright © 2011 by Michelle Celmer

www.Harlequin.com

Printed in U.S.A.

Books by Michelle Celmer

Harlequin Desire

Exposed: Her Undercover Millionaire #2084
†*One Month with the Magnate* #2099
†*A Clandestine Corporate Affair* #2106
†*Much More Than a Mistress* #2111

Silhouette Desire

Playing by the Baby Rules #1566
The Seduction Request #1626
Bedroom Secrets #1656
Round-the-Clock Temptation #1683
House Calls #1703
The Millionaire's Pregnant Mistress #1739
The Secretary's Secret #1774
Best Man's Conquest #1799
*The King's Convenient Bride #1876
*The Illegitimate Prince's Baby #1877
*An Affair with the Princess #1900
*The Duke's Boardroom Affair #1919
*Royal Seducer #1951
The Oilman's Baby Bargain #1970
*Christmas with the Prince #1979
Money Man's Fiancée Negotiation #2006
*Virgin Princess, Tycoon's Temptation #2026
*Expectant Princess, Unexpected Affair #2032
†*The Tycoon's Paternity Agenda* #2053

Harlequin Superromance

Nanny Next Door #1685

Silhouette Special Edition

Accidentally Expecting #1847

*Royal Seductions
†Black Gold Billionaires

MICHELLE CELMER

Bestselling author Michelle Celmer lives in southeastern Michigan with her husband, their three children, two dogs and two cats. When she's not writing or busy being a mom, you can find her in the garden or curled up with a romance novel. And if you twist her arm really hard, you can usually persuade her into a day of power shopping.

Michelle loves to hear from readers. Visit her website, www.michellecelmer.com, or write her at P.O. Box 300, Clawson, MI 48017.

To my Pumpkin Cookies

One

You can do this.

Jane Monroe walked from the parking lot to the front entrance of Western Oil's corporate headquarters, a legion of mutant butterflies doing the conga on her insides. She stopped just shy of the double glass doors and sucked in a breath of cool January air, flexing the jitters from her fingers.

In her first six months at Edwin Associates Investigation Services, she had logged hundreds of computer hours conducting background checks, tracking down deadbeat dads and finding assets hidden by cheating ex-husbands. When anyone needed legal advice, she was the woman to ask. And it had all been leading up to this very moment.

Her first undercover assignment.

Shivering from a combination of nerves and the brisk wind against her sheer nylons, she huddled down into her coat collar and wobbled into the lobby on four-inch heels.

She passed through the metal detectors, flashing the ID badge that would allow her to move freely throughout the building, even in areas reserved for the highest ranking employees.

She passed a bustling coffee shop on her way to the elevator, joining the flow of bodies as she stepped on, pressing the button for the third floor where she would report to Human Resources.

Some people, her parents and siblings in particular, would have considered her position at Edwin Associates a waste of her law degree. Which was why she hadn't exactly been honest about where she was working. They thought she was employed in the law department of a local corporation. It saved her a whole lot of headache that way. But when she cracked this case, and was made a full-fledged investigator, she could finally come clean.

How could they be anything but impressed to learn that she had been working undercover in the office of billionaire Jordan Everette, Chief Operations Officer of Western Oil, a man suspected of taking bribes and sabotage.

She won this case by default. The secretary she was replacing went into labor early, and the investigator who was supposed to be assigned to the case was stuck in another undercover position. It was her one and only chance to prove herself. She simply *could not* screw this up.

The agency was putting together a profile on Jane's target, but it wouldn't be messaged to her apartment until that evening. Until then, she would be flying blind. She'd never even seen a photo of her new "boss," much less met the man, but considering his position in the company she had already formed a mental picture. Late forties to early fifties, probably balding and thick around the middle from too many rich foods and malt scotch. A golf playing, cigar smoking man's man.

Jane tugged at the hem of the body-hugging, thigh-high skirt that was a complete departure from the conservative suits she normally wore. It had been assumed that a man like Mr. Everette, a confirmed bachelor who supposedly subscribed to the girl-of-the-month club, would be much more receptive to short skirts and spike heels than trousers and leather loafers. So she, the socially challenged geek who hadn't gone on her first real date until her second year of college, would be playing the role of the sexy temp secretary.

Even she hadn't been sure if she could pull it off, but after a weekend makeover that included a day in the stylist's chair, a crash course with a makeup artist, trading her glasses for contact lenses, and a trip to Macy's for a new work wardrobe, she was a little stunned to realize that she actually looked...sexy. When she'd stopped into work on her way to Western Oil to pick up her security badge, the girl at the front desk hadn't even recognized her, and heads had literally turned as she'd walked through the building to her boss's office.

She had driven to Western Oil feeling a confidence that was completely foreign to her. Right up until the second she stepped out of the car and let herself consider just how important this assignment could be.

Cracking this case would finally make her superiors take her seriously, and hopefully bring her that much closer to a corner office and an eventual partnership in what was a primarily male-dominated firm. Not only did she intend to be the first woman ever to make partner, but the youngest associate to climb the ranks as well.

More like *claw* her way up, she thought wryly, which

would be so much easier now with her new, siren-red acrylic nails.

The elevator stopped at the third floor and Jane walked down the hall to the HR office. She checked in at the desk and was told to take a seat. She took off her coat and sat in one of the hard plastic chairs. Only a few minutes passed before a sharply dressed, stern-looking older woman stepped into the waiting room. "Miss Monroe?"

Jane shot to her feet. Though undercover work often meant using an assumed name, for this particular position it was decided that she would stick as closely as possible to the actual details of her life. Not that she anticipated having deep and meaningful conversations with her new boss. But the fewer fabrications, the fewer she had to remember.

The woman gave Jane a quick once-over, one brow slightly raised, then shook her hand. "Welcome to Western Oil. I'm Mrs. Brown. I'll be showing you around. Would you follow me, please?"

Jane grabbed her coat and followed Mrs. Brown back down the hall to the elevator, her shoes pinching her toes to within an inch of their lives, making her long for a pair of her comfortable, low-heeled pumps.

"I'm assuming the temp agency gave you a copy of the office policies."

"Of course." In fact, she had memorized it. Other than Edwin Associates, Jane had never had a job outside of the family law practice. She'd worked there summers and after school since she was fourteen, and for five miserable years after getting her law degree before she'd had the guts to quit and follow her dream of being a P.I.

They stepped on the elevator and Mr. Brown hit the button for the top floor—the executive level—and Jane's heart climbed up into her throat. She was so nervous she could barely breathe. Or maybe the lack of oxygen was due to the underwire push-up bra digging into her rib cage.

The elevator opened to another security station.

"This is Miss Monroe," Mrs. Brown told the guard sitting there. "She'll be temping for Mr. Everette."

His badge said his name was Michael Weiss. He was twenty-something with military-short blond hair, built like a tank, and armed to the teeth.

"Welcome, Miss Monroe," he said with a nod, glancing subtly at her legs, which in the spiked heels looked miles longer than they actually were. At five feet seven inches no one could accuse her of being short, but now she felt like an Amazon. "Can I see your badge, please?"

She unclipped it from her lapel and handed it to him. He inspected it, jotted something on his clipboard, then handed it back. "Keep this clearly displayed at all times. You won't be allowed on the floor without it."

Security sure was tight. Understandably so, considering the combined net worth of the men working on that floor.

"This way," Mrs. Brown said, and as they walked through the double glass doors to the executive offices Jane could swear she felt the guard's gaze settle on her behind. She wasn't used to men looking at her butt, or any other part of her for that matter. Most men didn't give her so much as a passing glance. It was as if she was invisible— so drab and boring she faded into the woodwork. In high school the other kids called her "Plain Jane."

Not very original, but hurtful just the same. To finally be noticed was a little…exciting. Even if the woman people were noticing wasn't really her. Out of this costume she was the same old uninteresting Jane Monroe.

They entered another lobby area and stopped at the reception desk.

"This is Miss Monroe, Mr. Everette's temp," Mrs.

Brown told the woman sitting there, then she shot Jane a dismissive, borderline-hostile glance, and walked back out the door.

The woman behind the desk rolled her eyes and shook her head at Mrs. Brown's retreating form and mumbled in a thick Texas drawl, "Thank you, Miss Congeniality." She rose from her chair and smiled at Jane. She was short and cute, and on the plump side. "I'm Jen Walters. Welcome to the top floor, Miss Monroe."

"Hi Jen." Jane shook the hand she offered. "You can call me Jane."

She looked Jane up and down, shook her head and said, "Oh honey, the other girls are going to hate you."

Hate her? Her heart sank. "They hate all temps?"

"All temps who are as pretty as you are."

She opened her mouth to reply, but nothing came out. She didn't have a clue what to say. It was the first time in her life anyone accused her of being too pretty. And she had no idea why they would hate her for that.

Jen laughed and patted her arm. "I'm jokin', hon! They won't hate you. We're a friendly bunch up here."

That was a relief. She wasn't here to make friends, but it wouldn't be much fun working in a place where no one liked her.

"I'm really not that pretty," she told Jen.

Jen laughed again. "Do you not own a mirror? You're gorgeous. And I would kill for your figure. I'll bet you're one of those naturally skinny girls."

"If by naturally skinny you mean no bust or hips." And what breasts she did have hadn't come in until her senior year of high school.

She lowered her voice and said, "Take it from me, big boobs are not all they're cracked up to be."

Jane smiled, and realized that although she had walked

onto the floor trembling with nerves, Jen had put her completely at ease.

"Why don't I show you around and get you settled. Mr. Everette is in a meeting, but he should be out soon."

Jen showed her where the break room and restrooms were located, introduced her to the other secretaries on the floor—all of whom seemed very nice and did not seem to hate her—then showed her to her desk.

"Tiffany left you detailed instructions of your duties and how Mr. Everette likes things done," Jen told her, gesturing to the typed pages on the blotter next to a top-of-the-line flat-panel computer monitor. "She was hoping to be here to break in the temp, but her water broke at work two days ago. She wasn't due for another two weeks."

Jane looked at the chair, then back up at Jen. "Her water broke *here?*"

Jen laughed. "Not here in the office. She was walking from her car to the building."

Well, that was good. "I guess babies can be unpredictable like that," she said, not that she had any experience with them. Though both her brothers were married they hadn't started families yet, and like Jane, her sister was too career-oriented to even think about marriage, much less a baby. And being the baby of the family, Jane had no younger siblings.

"Mr. Everette's calls have been rerouted to my desk. I'll give you a couple of hours to get settled then have them sent to you."

"Thanks for showing me around," she said.

"Sure thing, honey. Call me if you have any questions. My number is in the office directory."

When she was gone, Jane peeked into her boss's office. Floor-to-ceiling windows lined two of the four sides, and overlooked the skyline of El Paso.

A corner office. Nice.

She hung her purse and coat in the closet then sat at her desk, setting her cell phone in the top drawer. She booted up the computer and unclipped the list Tiffany had typed up. It was pretty basic stuff—how Mr. Everette liked the phone answered, what he took in his coffee, who he took calls from on the spot and who was an auto callback—one being his mother, she noticed. Nothing she couldn't handle easily. There was also a list of numbers that included his housecleaning service, his laundry service and reservation lines for a dozen of the finest restaurants in the greater El Paso area. Clearly she would be handling some of the personal aspects of his life as well as the professional, which could only work in her favor.

She considered going through the files on the computer, on the very rare possibility that there might be something there to incriminate him, but as she ran her tongue across her upper lip, she realized that in her nervousness, she'd chewed off all of her lipstick. It probably wouldn't be a bad idea to freshen up before her boss came in.

She grabbed her purse and headed down the hall to the ladies' room. As she suspected, her lipstick was pretty much gone, so she drew on a fresh layer then gave her face a light dusting with the mineral powder the makeup artist swore by. It did give her skin a smooth, almost ethereal look. Although at twenty-eight—make that twenty-nine tomorrow—she wasn't exactly covered in wrinkles. But it did cover the freckles that had been the bane of her existence since middle school. It had been hard enough being two years younger than her classmates, and even worse looking it. She never imagined makeup could make such a difference in the way she looked. She had tried it once before. She was an awkward and geeky twelve-year-old, and had gotten into the makeup case her sister had left in the bathroom that they shared. Thinking she had done a pretty good job, she showed her sister, who had dissolved into hysterics at how ridiculous she looked. Then she had dragged Jane in front of their brothers who also laughed at her. She ran sobbing to her mother, who, instead of offering comfort, told Jane she had to toughen up, and face the fact that some girls just didn't look good wearing makeup. And as a former Miss Texas, her mother knew a thing or two about fashion and beauty.

It was the first and last time Jane ever tried that.

She didn't doubt that she'd probably looked a bit like a clown, but instead of pulling her aside and trying to teach her the right way, her sister had felt the need to boost her own ego—which was as overinflated then as it was today—and ridicule Jane instead.

She finished her face, studied her reflection, and smiled. She did look really nice. But she wouldn't get much work done if she spent the day gazing at her reflection in the bathroom mirror.

She stopped in the break room to grab a cup of coffee, then headed back to her desk. When she walked through the door and realized someone was already sitting there, she stopped so abruptly she sloshed coffee onto her fingers.

Thinking she must have walked into the wrong office by mistake, she shot a quick glance to the the name on the door, but this was definitely the right place. So who was the man sitting at her desk?

He was lounging back in her chair, his designer shoe—clad feet propped on the desk surface, reading the list Tiffany had left. He wore typical office attire, sans the jacket, and the sleeves of his dress shirt were rolled to his elbows. His hair was dark blond and stylishly short, and he had the sort of boyish good looks that made a girl swoon. Which was exactly what she felt like doing.

The question was, who was he and why he was in her office?

"Can I help you?" she asked.

The man looked up at her with a pair of deep-set, soul-warming hazel eyes and a grin that could stop traffic, and her heart actually flipped over in her chest. Who *was* this guy and where could she get one?

"I certainly hope so," he said, dropping his feet to the carpet and rising from the chair. She was at least 5'11" in her heels and she had to look up to meet his eyes. He was tall and lean and work-out-in-the-gym-every-morning fit.

"You must be the new temp," he said, reaching across the desk to shake her hand, which was still gripping the cup of coffee and damp from the sloshing. She quickly switched the cup to the opposite hand, wiped the damp one on her skirt and took his hand. It was big and warm and surprisingly rough for such a polished-looking guy.

His grip was firm and confident and she could swear she felt the effects all the way to her knees. She also didn't miss the way he gave her a quick once-over, one brow slightly raised.

"I'm Jane Monroe," she said.

"It's a pleasure to meet you, Jane Monroe."

No, the pleasure was definitely hers, though she still didn't have clue who he was.

"By the way," he said. "Someone named Mary called."

Her heart stalled. Her *sister* Mary? How could she possibly have known where Jane was working? Her family didn't even know she was working for Edwin Associates. "She called *here?*"

"Your cell," he said, opening the top drawer and holding up her cell phone.

"You answered my phone?" Who the hell did this guy

think he was? And how could she be so stupid as to leave it unattended in her desk with the ringer on?

"Actually, it went to voice mail before I found it in the drawer. But the display said it was Mary."

Whoever this guy was, he had a lot of nerve. "Do you make it a habit of snooping through people's private property?"

He shrugged. "Only if I think I'll find something interesting."

That was not the answer she expected. "Who *are* you?"

"You don't know?"

"Should I?"

The smile went from curious to amused. "I'm Jordan Everette, Miss Monroe. Your new boss."

Two

"M-Mr. Everette," Miss Monroe stammered, the color draining from her flawlessly painted face. "I'm so sorry. I didn't realize—"

"Not quite what you expected, I guess," Jordan said.

She shook her head, pulling her full bottom lip between her teeth.

Well, neither was she. In fact, he was surprised that anyone had shown up at all.

"So, the temp agency sent you?" he asked.

"That's right."

Funny, he had called the agency Friday afternoon to see what was taking so long—usually they had a temp to his office within hours of the request—but they had no record of a request ever being submitted. Yet here she was, bright and early Monday morning, standing in his office.

For a couple of weeks now there had been a strange vibe in the office. Something was just…*off*. He could only assume that the focus of the investigation into the explosion at the refinery had now moved from his employees to him.

After six years of loyal service, and three as Chief Operations Officer, he would have thought Adam Blair, Western Oil's current CEO, would trust him by now. And if they had concerns, why not just ask him? Why this elaborate charade?

Because if they mistrusted him enough to think he could do this sort of thing—put his workers' lives in jeopardy—they probably didn't think he would tell the truth if confronted. So instead they hired someone to do what? Seduce it out of him? He couldn't imagine another reason they would send a woman who looked as though she moonlighted as a runway model.

Did they really think he was that shallow?

They obviously thought a lot less of him than he did of them. He would have at least hoped that his brother Nathan, the Chief Brand Officer, would come clean and tell him the truth. If he even knew, that is. Hell, for all Jordan knew Adam could be investigating him too. Maybe even Emilio Suarez, the CFO.

The weight of the betrayal sat like a stone in his gut, but his options were limited. He could confront Adam and put an end to the investigation, but that might only make him appear as if he had something to hide. He couldn't let anything, not even his pride, interfere with his chance at the coveted CEO position Adam would be vacating soon. His only choice was to cooperate with their investigation.

Of course, that didn't mean he was going to make it easy for his new "secretary." Knowing who she was and why she was there, he could manipulate the situation, control the information she obtained. Let her see only what he wanted her to see. Not that they were going to find anything incriminating, because he hadn't done anything wrong. But there were certain aspects of his life—financial ones in particular—that he preferred to keep private.

"Here," Jordan said, backing away from her chair. "Have a seat."

Smiling nervously, Miss Monroe rounded the desk. "Can I get you a cup of coff—" The toe of one spike-heeled "do-me" shoe caught on the desk leg and she lurched forward. She grabbed the corner of the desk in her attempt to catch her fall, but the foam cup she was holding in the opposite hand went airborne. And hit him square in the chest.

Miss Monroe gasped in horror, slapping a hand over her crimson-painted mouth as coffee soaked not only his shirt, but the carpet where he was standing. "Oh my God. I can't believe I just did that."

She looked frantically around for something to clean up the mess and spotted a box of tissues on the desk. She lunged for it, ripping out a handful and shoving them at him. "Mr. Everette, I am *so* sorry."

"It's okay," he said, wiping up the coffee dripping from his chin. Not the most graceful runway model, was she?

She gestured helplessly at his damp shirt. "Is there anything I can do?"

"I keep an extra shirt in the closet for emergencies. You could grab it for me while I clean up."

"Of course," she said, scrambling for the closet.

Jordan walked to the bathroom in his office, unbuttoning his shirt. Some of the coffee had hit his pants too, but as luck would have it, he'd worn his brown suit that morning.

He dropped his shirt on the bathroom floor, and peeled his coffee-soaked undershirt over his head. Maybe she wasn't an agency operative after all. Or was this just all part of a clever disguise? A ruse to throw him off the trail?

"Mr. Everette?" she called from his office.

"In here." He wet a washcloth in the sink and wiped the coffee from his face and chest.

"Here's your…"

Jordan turned to see Miss Monroe in the bathroom doorway, eyes wide and fixed somewhere between his neck and his belt. She blinked and quickly looked away, a red hue creeping up from the neckline of her blouse. Why would an above-average-looking woman who practically oozed sexuality blush at the sight of a shirtless man?

Interesting.

Eyes averted, she held out the hanger with his clean shirt. "Here you go."

He took it, brushing his fingers against hers as he did, and she jerked her hand away.

Very interesting.

"Are you going to fire me?" she asked.

Why bother? They would just send a new agency person in.

"Did you do it on purpose?" he asked.

She blinked in surprise and cut her eyes to him. "Of course not!"

He hooked the hanger on the towel rack, tugged the clean undershirt free and pulled it over his head. "Then why would I fire you?"

She pulled her lip between her teeth again, and it brought to mind nibbling on a plump red cherry. He wondered if she had the slightest clue how sexy she looked when she did that. The coy bit had to be an act.

He pulled on his shirt and buttoned it. "In answer to your question, yes."

"My question?"

"I would love a cup of coffee. Although this time I'd rather not wear it."

Her lips tilted into an embarrassed smile. "Of course."

"My cup is on my desk." He unfastened his belt and the button on his pants so he could tuck in his shirt, stifling a grin when she quickly looked away again.

"I—I'll go get it now," she said, tripping over her own foot in her haste to get away.

He had the feeling that, until she discovered that the evidence she was hoping to find didn't exist and gave up, he could have an awful lot of fun at her expense.

The spike heels had been a really bad idea, Jane decided as she grabbed Mr. Everette's *World's Best Boss* cup from his desk and hurried to the break room, heart pounding from a combination of her own horrifying ineptitude and supreme lack of grace, and the sight of her new boss standing shamelessly bare-chested in her presence.

Not that he had *anything* to be ashamed of. His body— what she could see of it anyway—was a work of art. And she was betting that the bottom half was no less awe-inspiring. So much for her theory that he was middle-aged and fat. That's what she got for drawing hasty conclusions.

Some vampy, sex goddess secretary she'd turned out to be. She couldn't have made more of an ass out of herself if she'd dressed like a clown and donned a squeaky red nose. Proof that despite her physical transformation, deep down she was just as geeky and awkward as ever. Had she been completely fooling herself to believe that she could handle an undercover position?

She poured the coffee and added a teaspoon of creamer, mentally shaking away those negative thoughts. She could do this, damn it. She *was* good enough. She had been working up to this for months. Failure was not an option.

Squaring her shoulders, she carried the coffee back to Mr. Everette's office. She rapped lightly on the door before stepping inside, grateful to see that he was fully clothed and sitting at his desk. He was also on the phone, meaning she didn't have to talk to him. It was both a disappointment and a relief. If she was going to glean the information necessary for the investigation, she was going to have to talk to the man. Get to know him. Earn his trust.

He gestured her over, telling the caller, "I'm sure it was just an oversight."

She crossed the room, the cup cradled gingerly in both palms, and set it on his desk. She started to turn, but he held up a hand, signaling her to wait. "Yes, Mother, I promise I'll talk to him today." He paused, looking exasperated, then said, "Well, in all fairness, you ditched us on Christmas. Can you blame Nathan if he's feeling bitter?"

She could only assume he was talking about his brother Nathan, who was the CBO of Western Oil. Having worked closely with her own siblings for years, she knew how complicated the family dynamic could be. Especially when one broke tradition and made the decision to leave the fold to pursue their own aspirations. Not that she had a clue how the Everette family got along. Although most men in a decent relationship with their mother wouldn't have them on an auto callback list.

"The fact that he was a baron doesn't make it okay," he said, holding up a finger to indicate that it would be just one more minute. "I have to go, Mother, I—" He rolled his eyes. "Yes, I *will* talk to him. I promise." Another short pause then, "Okay, Mother. *Goodbye.*" He hung up the phone, blew out an exasperated breath and looked up at Jane. "Do you get along with your mother, Miss Monroe?"

The question threw her, and it took her a second to regroup. It wasn't that she didn't get along with her parents. They just refused to accept that they didn't know what was better for her than she did. And she couldn't help wondering why he cared about her relationship with her mother. "It's…complicated."

"Well, mine is a gigantic pain in the ass. She's a master manipulator and will browbeat you to within an inch of your life to get what she wants. You have to be firm and direct or she will walk all over you."

"I understand," she said, although firm and direct were never two of her strong suits. Her own family had been walking all over her for years. But she had broken the cycle, hadn't she? Well, for the most part anyway. She tended to just avoid them now. And, yes, bent the truth when it made her life easier.

"Would you mind pouring that coffee into a travel mug?" he asked. "There should be one in the cabinet over by the wet bar."

"Of course." She carried his cup to the bar across the room, asking casually, "Are you leaving?"

"I have a meeting at the refinery."

That would give her time to snoop in his office. Her heart surged with nervous energy. She found the cup where he'd indicated and as she poured the coffee in, her hands were shaking.

Relax, she told herself, taking a deep breath.

She could just imagine how impressed her superiors would be if she were able to bring them valuable information on her very first day. Then they would *have* to take her seriously.

It took a couple of tries but she secured the top on the cup and turned, jerking with surprise when she almost ran face-first into Mr. Everette. He was so close, she could smell the soapy-fresh scent of his skin. If the cup hadn't had a lid, they would probably both be wearing coffee this time.

"Sorry, didn't mean to startle you," he said, but the

grin he wore said otherwise. Was he *teasing* her? Were the makeup and the clothes actually working?

He took the cup from her, the tips of his fingers brushing against hers as he did and she tried not to flinch. He set it on the counter beside the sink. "I think we'd all be safer if you didn't carry that around."

She felt herself blushing. "Sorry."

With a grin that was nothing short of adorable, he stepped past her to the closet next to the bathroom and pulled out his coat.

"Is there anything you need me to do while you're gone?" she asked as he shrugged into it.

"Just man the phones and take the day to get settled in. Familiarize yourself with the computer. I have a lunch meeting at twelve-thirty so I should be back sometime before two."

Which would give her lots of time to snoop. No, not snoop...*investigate*. She had to start·thinking like a pro, using the appropriate lingo. She had to play the part, even in her own mind. If she didn't take herself seriously, no one would.

"I should take you out sometime," he said.

She blinked. Did he seriously just ask her on a date? And how was she supposed to respond to that? What would a sophisticated woman of the world say?

All she could manage was a befuddled, "Um..."

"I'm assuming you've never been to a refinery."

Oh, he wanted to take her to the *refinery*. That made a lot more sense. "No, never."

"It's an impressive operation," he said, and she must have looked wary, because he added, "and contrary to what you've probably seen on the news, it's completely safe."

She had heard negative press about the incident at the refinery, but the agency had several employees working undercover directly on the line, and as far as she was aware, none of them had ever reported being in any danger. Sure, this was a high-profile case, but the other agents would never be sent into a situation that could cause them physical harm.

"I'd love to see it," she said.

"I'm there several days a week, so maybe the next time I go." He glanced at the platinum Rolex on his left wrist. "I'm late. If there's anything pressing while I'm gone, or something you aren't sure about, feel free to call my cell."

"I will." She handed him his cup, careful to avoid his fingers this time because frankly, she was nervous enough without all the intimate contact.

Cup in hand, he headed for the door. She followed him, stopping at her desk.

"By the way," he said, stopping in the doorway and gesturing the coffee stain on the carpet. "Call janitorial to take care of that."

"I will." *Later.*

He flashed her one last knee-melting smile, then left. *Here we go.*

She stood there and counted to sixty, gauging the amount of time it would take him to get to the elevator and get inside, then she walked down the hall. The elevator doors were just closing as she stepped into the reception area.

"Did Mr. Everette leave yet?" she asked Jen.

"You just missed him, hon."

"Well, darn," she said, pretending to be discouraged.

"Did he forget something?" She put her hand on the phone. "Should I call down to the guard post in the lobby?"

"That's okay. It's nothing urgent. I just had a question, but it can wait until he gets back." It was a lie, of course. She just needed to be sure that he was really gone.

Jen smiled. "How's the first day going so far?"

With the exception of dumping hot coffee on her new boss and making a complete ass out of herself? "Pretty good."

"If you're interested, the secretaries are all going out for lunch today. You're welcome to join us."

She was inclined to say no, since she wanted to take as much time as possible in Mr. Everette's office, but she didn't want the other secretaries to think she was a snob either. She might learn something valuable from any one of them. Things that they may not even realize were important to the investigation.

She smiled and said, "I'd love to go. What time?"

"Noon. There's a café across the street. Just a few minutes' walk. The temperature is supposed to climb to forty, so it shouldn't be too cold."

"Sounds great," she said, cringing inwardly. It wasn't the cold she was worried about, but her aching feet. She should have brought a pair of flat shoes as a backup.

Jen smiled. "Great, see you at noon."

Jane walked back to the desk and kicked off her shoes. She wanted to be able to move quickly, in case someone happened to come by. If someone did, and they asked what she was doing in Mr. Everette's office, she would simply say that she'd spilled coffee on her jacket and was using the fabric stain remover she had seen on his bathroom shelf.

She opened the closet and rifled through her purse for the jump drive that Kenneth in Tech had given her at her briefing that morning. She was just hoping Mr. Everette's computer wasn't password protected. She doubted he would have any personal financial files at work, but she could at least get a look at his email. People sent personal emails from work all the time.

She slipped the jump drive in her pocket, heart pounding

with both fear and excitement, and turned toward Mr. Everette's office, but before she could take a step, the phone started to ring.

Damn it!

She picked it up. "Good morning, Mr. Everette's office."

"Miss Monroe, this is Bren, in Mr. Blair's office. He'd like a word with you."

Her heart jumped. Why would the CEO want to see her? Had she done something wrong?

Of course she hadn't. Other than the coffee fiasco, that is, and unless they had a surveillance camera in her office, there was no way he could have found out about that. Maybe he just wanted to talk to her about the case. "I'll be right down."

She took the jump drive from her pocket and slipped it in the top drawer of her desk, crammed her feet back into her shoes and walked down to Mr Blair's office at the opposite end of the hall.

"Go on in," Mr. Blair's secretary said. "They're waiting for you."

Jane stopped so abruptly she wobbled on her heels. *"They?"*

"Mr. Blair, Mr. Suarez and Mr. Everette." She paused and said, "The *other* Mr. Everette."

Suddenly Jane was having a tough time pulling in a full breath.

She thought she was just meeting with the CEO, which was intimidating enough. But to be in the same room with the CEO, CFO and CBO all at the same time? No wonder she felt faint. Meeting clients as a lawyer had never been a big deal, but then, she knew the law so well she could practice it in her sleep. The investigation business…not so much. She was still learning, and there was nothing she hated more than looking as though she didn't know what she was talking about.

Bren must have sensed that she was on the verge of a panic attack because she flashed Jane a reassuring smile and said, "Don't worry, they don't bite."

Jane tried to smile, when what she wanted to do was turn and run in the opposite direction.

"I'm sure they just want to ask you about the investigation."

Jane blinked. "The what?"

"It's okay, Miss Monroe. What Mr. Blair knows, I know."

Mr. Blair obviously trusted his secretary implicitly, which could definitely work in Jane's favor.

"You know," Bren said, lowering her voice, "we all like and respect Mr. Everette, and no one wants to believe he could have anything to with the sabotage. The sooner this investigation is over with, the better. If there's anything I can do to help, just say the word."

"Thanks. And we'll get to the bottom of this," she told Bren, hoping to convey a competence she was nowhere close to feeling.

Jane turned to the door, pulled back her shoulders, and took a deep breath. "Well, I guess I'd better get in there."

Bren smiled and said, "Good luck."

Considering that her knees were actually knocking, she had the feeling she was probably going to need it.

Three

Like Mr. Everette, Mr. Blair had a corner office, but it was nearly twice the size and much more luxurious. Mr. Blair, whom she recognized from the television news stories that had run after the refinery explosion, sat behind his desk. He was dark-haired, conservatively handsome, and the touch of gray at his temples said he was probably in his early forties.

"Miss Monroe," he said, rising from his chair, as did the man seated across from his desk. A third man stood by the window. "Come in. Close the door behind you."

She did as he asked and crossed the room, hands trembling, palms sweaty, praying she didn't trip and make a total fool of herself. Her toes were pinched so tight in her shoes that each step was torture.

Good lord, she was a wreck. She could only hope she didn't look half as terrified as she felt.

"Miss Monroe, I'm Adam Blair, and this is Nathan

Everette, our Chief Brand Officer." Mr. Blair indicated the man by his desk, then he turned to the one by the window and said, "And this is Emilio Suarez, our Chief Financial Officer."

She nodded to both men, who each gave her a very subtle once-over. Nathan Everette was darker than his brother, and a little larger in stature, but there was a strong family resemblance. Mr. Suarez was the utter epitome of tall, dark and handsome and of Hispanic descent. All three men were above-average in the looks department and she nearly felt faint from the ridiculously high level of testosterone in the room. She wondered if looking like a *GQ* cover model was prerequisite to their positions.

"Please, have a seat," Mr. Blair said, indicating the chair next to Mr. Everette.

She sat primly on the edge. Mr. Blair and Mr. Everette both took their seats while Mr. Suarez remained standing, arms crossed, his expression dark. As an attorney, she had gotten pretty good at reading people and situations, and there was a definite negative vibe in the room.

"First off, I'd like to make it clear that none of us are happy about the need to investigate our colleague," Mr. Blair said. "Your boss has assured me that this will be handled with the utmost care."

"Absolutely," she said, hoping they didn't hear the quiver in her voice.

Mr. Blair leaned forward in his seat, folding his hands atop his desk. "He told me that the plan is for you to get to know Mr. Everette on a more...*personal* level. To be honest, I'm not sure I'm comfortable with that."

Okay. Well, that was very...direct. She had barely begun the investigation and already they were unhappy.

She was so completely screwed.

She squared her shoulders and tried to sound as if

she knew what she was talking about. "If Mr. Everette is involved in a conspiracy, chances are slim he would be foolish enough to keep any incriminating evidence at work. More than likely I'll need access to his home."

"And you'll do that how?" Mr. Suarez asked. He didn't outwardly suggest impropriety, but the implication was there. She tried not to take it personally. Actually, she felt sort of sorry for them. They were clearly distressed by what they had to do.

"It's against agency policy to engage in activity that is illegal or unethical," she told him.

Mr. Everette rubbed his forehead, looking pained. "I don't like it."

"Two weeks ago you and Jordan weren't on speaking terms," Mr. Suarez said.

Mr. Everette shot him a look. "It just seems so... underhanded. That doesn't bother you?"

"Of course it bothers me. And if it were one of my brothers being investigated I would probably be just as hesitant. But, Nathan, we don't have a choice. We *need* to know, and we agreed this was the best way to handle the situation."

"You all seem to respect Mr. Everette," she said. "Why is it that you think he could have been the saboteur?"

"As you probably already know, a week before the explosion someone wired two hundred thousand dollars into Jordan's account, and a few days later he wired thirty thousand dollars out. But we don't know where the money came from, or who it went to."

"So you think that someone paid him, and he paid someone else to tamper with the equipment."

"That's one possibility," Adam said.

"Why? I've seen his financials. He's not hurting for money."

"Jordan is ambitious," Adam said. "This happened before everyone learned the CEO position was opening up. Maybe he felt he'd hit a ceiling. Maybe someone made him an offer he couldn't refuse, but expected something in return first."

"And you believe he would put people's lives in danger to further his career?" she asked.

"Maybe no one was meant to get hurt, but something went wrong," Emilio suggested.

"If you're right, and he got a better offer, why is he still here?"

"To avoid suspicion? Or maybe now that the CEO position is opening up, he has a reason to stay."

"Or maybe," Emilio offered, "since there were injuries, it killed the deal."

All plausible scenarios. Especially if he was as ambitious as they all seemed to believe.

"That's what we need you to find out," Mr. Blair said, looking to Mr Everette. "And either we're all in, or this stops today."

Jane held her breath. Would her first undercover assignment be over before it started? If she blew this on the very first day, would her boss blame her? They might never give her another chance to work undercover. She needed to take the bull by the horns.

"Mr. Everette," she said, reaching out to touch his arm, hoping he couldn't sense her desperation. "I have three siblings myself, so I understand how difficult this must be for you. I'll take whatever steps necessary to ensure that no one is hurt. You have my word."

Mr. Everette glanced from her to his partners, looking conflicted. For a second she thought for sure he would refuse to cooperate, but he finally sighed and said, "Okay, lets do it."

Jane breathed a silent sigh of relief. That was a close one.

Mr. Blair stood, which she took to mean that the meeting was over. She rose from her seat, her achy feet screaming in protest.

"If you need anything from us, don't hesitate to ask," he said. "We would like this resolved as soon as possible."

Nodding to each man, she said, "It was a pleasure to meet you, gentlemen," then she turned and walked to the door, praying she didn't trip on anything, and let herself out of the office, limp with relief. That had gone *way* better than she expected.

"Well?" Bren asked as Jane snapped the door shut behind her. She held up her thumb in an "okay" gesture, startled when the door opened behind her and Mr. Everette stepped out.

"My office, *now*," he told Jane, and her heart immediately sank. Oh hell. Maybe the worst of it wasn't over after all.

She followed him across the hall, knees knocking again. At this rate she was going to need a straightjacket before the day was over.

"Lynn, hold my calls," he told his secretary, who looked surprised to see him with his brother's secretary. Jane wondered if he realized that a move like this could very well blow her cover.

He gestured her into his office and stepped in behind her, closing the door. She actually flinched as it snapped shut. Was it possible that despite what he'd told his partners, he still wasn't okay with the investigation? Did he intend on giving her a hard time?

He crossed the room to his desk and sat down. "Have a seat, Miss Monroe."

She did as he asked, sitting on the edge of the chair across from his desk.

"In the interest of getting this investigation resolved as quickly as possible, there are a few things I should tell you about my brother."

He wanted to *help* her? "Yes, please. Anything you think would be helpful."

"I can only assume the agency is aware of my brother's reputation as a womanizer, and that's why they sent you."

"That was the idea."

"Well, I'm sure you've caught his attention. You're a very beautiful woman Miss Monroe, and please don't take this the wrong way, but it's going to take more than a pretty face and a tight skirt to *keep* him interested."

Take it the wrong way? A gorgeous billionaire just called her beautiful and he thought she would be *offended*? If her feet weren't so darned sore she might be turning cartwheels across his office.

"Do you have any advice as to what *will* keep him interested?"

"My brother loves a challenge, so don't make it too easy for him. If you're too aggressive, he'll lose interest. Make him work for it. Play hard to get."

Considering her pathetic lack of experience chasing the opposite sex, she liked the idea of letting Mr. Everette come to her.

"Also, he'll find you measurably more appealing if you make it clear that you have no interest in any sort of commitment."

She could definitely do that.

"But probably the most important thing to keep in mind is that my brother has a short attention span when it comes to the opposite sex. He'll have expectations, and if they aren't met, he'll get bored pretty fast."

Then she would have to work quickly. Because if he was talking about what she thought he was talking about, meeting *those* expectations was not even an option. She wanted to crack this case, but even she had limits. And even if she was that desperate, if her boss learned that she had slept with the subject of an investigation to get information, her career would be over.

"I'll be honest, Miss Monroe. My brother and I don't exactly see eye to eye on most things. The truth is, he can be an arrogant ass, but he's not a bad person."

"You protect him."

He sighed and leaned back in his chair. "For the life of me I don't know why."

"Because that's what big brothers do. I know, I have two of them." Although in her case, they didn't just protect. They domineered.

Mr. Everette smiled. He wasn't nearly as intimidating as she'd first thought. At first glance he seemed so dark and intense, but he definitely had a softer side. "With a sister as pretty as you, I'm sure it was a full-time job."

Wow, she really liked this guy.

"Well," he said, rising from his chair. "I'm glad we had this talk. But I should let you get back to work."

She stood and smoothed her skirt back into place. "Thank you for the advice."

He reached across the desk to shake her hand. His grip was firm and confident. "Good luck, Miss Monroe."

She left Nathan Everette's office feeling a lot less unsure of herself than when she'd walked into work that morning. The first day of her first undercover assignment may have had a bit of a bumpy start, but things were definitely looking up.

She hobbled back to her desk on her poor tortured feet, yet she felt a renewed confidence. If she could maintain her cool in a meeting with the CEO, CBO and CFO of a multibillion dollar corporation, she could handle just about anything.

When she got there she kicked off her shoes and opened her top drawer, fishing out the flash drive. It was time to go get some information.

"Is it my imagination or were you a lot taller the last time I saw you?"

At the sound of Mr. Everette's voice she gasped in surprise and dropped the flash drive back in the drawer. She whipped around, slamming it shut with her backside. He stood in his office doorway, arms folded, leaning against the jamb. And he must have been back for some time because not only was his coat off, he'd removed his suit jacket as well. "You're back early."

"I made it as far as the lobby and got a call that the meeting was cancelled."

If she hadn't been called away, he would have without a doubt walked in on her "investigating." The thought made her knees go weak. Next time she would have to make sure that he'd actually left the building before she set foot in his office.

"Imagine my surprise when I returned to find that my new secretary was already playing hooky."

"N-no...I wasn't..." She stopped and took a deep breath. What was the point of making excuses. "I'm sorry, it won't happen again."

"Where were you?"

Okay, she could handle this. It was all about thinking on her feet, and being prepared. So of course her mind went instantly blank. "The, um...HR office."

"Human resources?"

"Yes."

"For...?"

"Paperwork. There was a form they forgot to have me sign."

"And they stole your shoes while you were there?" he said, nodding to her stocking feet.

"No, of course not. They're under my desk. They're new and they were pinching my toes." At least that much was the truth. "I can put them back on—"

"Oh no. I wouldn't want to be responsible for your sore feet. Although maybe they would hurt less if you sat down."

She lowered herself into her chair.

"I need to go talk to my brother," he said, and before she could stop herself she sucked in a breath. Did he know she'd just been there?

No, of course he didn't. How could he?

He gave her an odd look. "Problem?"

She gestured to her feet. "Sorry, sore toes."

"As I was saying, I have to talk to my brother before my mother blows a gasket. But if anyone calls, I'm in a meeting."

"Of course."

With one last curious look her way, he walked out.

The man must have thought she was a loon.

Her cell phone started to ring and she pulled it out of the desk drawer, where she had left it again.

And it was her sister, Mary. Again. She pressed the talk button. "Hey Mary, what's up?"

"You sure are tough to get ahold of," Mary snapped in lieu of a hello.

Jane sighed. She had half a mind to just hang up on her. She wished she had the guts to do it, but things had been so strained lately already, she didn't want to make it worse. Mary was just pissy because Jane was no longer around the office to do her grunt work. Despite having graduated with higher honors than every one of her siblings, and passing the bar with flying colors, up until the day Jane had left, they had continued to treat her like an intern.

"I'm at work. I haven't had a chance to call you back."

"Whatever," she said, sounding like a spoiled adolescent. Though she was the older sister, she didn't always act like it. "I'm just calling to remind you about this Friday."

"What about it?"

She sighed dramatically. "Monthly dinner with the family, stupid."

Jane ignored the "stupid" remark, because although Mary may have been prettier, and more outgoing and popular, they both knew Jane was smarter. Though sometimes that was more of a liability than a asset. Being the "smart and practical" sibling didn't leave a lot of room for error.

"But we usually do that the last Friday of the month," she told her sister. "That's not until next week."

"Don't you remember, we decided to do it a week early because Will has a business trip the following week."

"That's news to me," she said.

"I could swear we talked about it."

"Nope." But then, since she'd left the practice, there were a lot of things she didn't hear about until the last minute because no one bothered to call her. She figured it was probably her punishment for deviating from their master plan.

"I'm sure I told you, but whatever. Mom booked our regular table at Via Penna. Seven o'clock."

"I'll try to be there."

"You'll *try*? What is your problem? You can't even make time for your family anymore?"

"Jeez, Mary, don't have a cow. I'll definitely be there, okay?"

"I'll see you Friday," she said, then hung up without saying goodbye.

Jane grumbled to herself and tossed her phone back into the drawer, then pulled it back out, walked to the closet and dropped it into her purse. It didn't occur to her until several minutes later that since her birthday was the following day, they were probably planning a party. That was probably the reason they were doing it a week early. No wonder Mary had been so insistent on her being there.

It didn't excuse the curt conversation, or Mary's bitchy attitude, but it made Jane feel a little better. And a little less like punching her sister in the nose the next time she saw her.

Four

Grinning to himself, Jordan walked down the hall to his brother's office. He had to hand it to Miss Monroe, she was quick on her feet.

He had figured there was a good chance when he came back early from the meeting, that he himself had cancelled, he would catch Miss Monroe snooping around. He was curious to see what sort of excuse she could come up with, and he was disappointed to not find her in his office. She wasn't at her desk either. It had taken one call down to his brother's secretary Lynn to learn that Miss Monroe had first been in Adam's office, then Nathan's. Until that moment Jordan had held out the hope that maybe his brother didn't know Adam was having him investigated. Not much chance of that now.

"I just need a minute," Jordan told Lynn when he reached Nathan's office. Then, as usual, instead of waiting to be announced, he walked right in. Mostly because he knew it would irritate the hell out of Nathan.

And it did. He jerked with surprise and said, "Jesus, Jordan, don't you ever knock?"

He had been reading something in a manila file and shut it quickly as Jordan approached his desk. Making Jordan instantly suspicious.

"Tell me you didn't deliberately forget to send our mother an invitation to your wedding."

Nathan sighed. "I take it she called you."

"Of course she called me. She's very upset."

He shrugged. "And I'm supposed to care *why?*"

Sometimes Jordan got so sick of being the go-between with Nathan and their parents. "Nathan, come on."

"To be honest, I didn't think she would care if she was invited or not."

"Well, apparently she does. She said she hasn't even seen Max yet." Max was the infant son Nathan hadn't even known he had until recently. He was the result of an affair Nathan had with the daughter of the owner of a rival oil company. If there was one thing Jordan could say about his brother, he liked to live on the edge, although lately he'd begun to act like a full-fledged family man.

"Did she happen to mention that I invited her over to meet Ana and Max last week, but something more important came up and she called it off at the last minute?"

"No, she left that part out." That was typical of their mother. Both the calling off and the leaving out part. She would say pretty much anything to make herself the victim.

"She had her chance," Nathan said. "I'm through catering to her whims. And for the life of me, I don't know why you still put up with it."

Neither did he. He wasn't going to deny that their mother was self-absorbed and narcissistic. That said, she was the only mother they had. And there was still a tiny part of him, a shadow of the awkward little boy who would do practically anything to win her attention.

"She sounded genuinely upset," he said.

Nathan's expression was deadpan. "My heart bleeds for her."

"Maybe she realizes that if she ever wants to see one of her sons get married, this might be her only chance. And possibly her only chance for grandchildren."

"She doesn't care about Max. She's already warned me that when he starts talking he is forbidden from calling her grandma. She said it would make her feel too old."

Jordan winced. "I'm sure she'll feel differently when she gets closer to him," he said, although honestly, he didn't know if even he believed that. Their mother hadn't had much of an interest in her own sons when they were small. They interfered too much with her social life. He and Nathan were raised primarily by the nanny.

But sometimes people were more open to the idea of children when it was someone else's child. Jordan was in no way, shape or form ready to have children of his own, and probably never would be, but he liked to tussle with little Max. He could have the fun without the responsibility.

"This has nothing to do with me getting married, or Max. She's just pissed off because she knows I invited Dad."

Jordan's jaw actually dropped. Until a few weeks ago, Nathan and their father hadn't spoken a word to each other in almost ten years, and Jordan had been on both their backs for ages, trying to persuade them to reconnect. Jordan understood why Nathan was hesitant. He and their father had a pretty volatile relationship, one that had often turned physically violent. But that was a long time ago and their father had mellowed since then. He also felt a lot of guilt and regret for the way that he'd treated Nathan. And though Jordan would never admit it, especially to Nathan, he felt his own share of guilt.

When they were kids, Jordan had been a late bloomer and Nathan had taken it upon himself to act as Jordan's protector. Instead of teaching Jordan to defend himself, Nathan took the knocks for him. It left Jordan feeling weak, small and resentful of his older brother. In rebellion he began getting Nathan in trouble on purpose, setting him up, knowing their father would take it out of his hide. It had, for a time, left Nathan with some serious anger management issues. Only recently, when Nathan nearly gave up his son because of it, did Jordan realize how deeply his manipulating had affected his brother.

Actually inviting their father to the wedding was a huge step for Nathan. Jordan had begun to think that maybe it was time he and Nathan began to repair their own relationship, time that they let go of the resentment. But now with the sabotage, and the accusations…well, it could be a while before they resolved anything.

"I think it's great that you invited him," Jordan said.

Nathan shrugged, like it wasn't a big deal. "Ana insisted."

Ana could insist until she was blue, but Nathan wouldn't have done it unless he wanted to. "And would it really be so terrible to invite Mom, too?"

"I put up with her crap for years because besides you, she was the only family I had. Well, I have my own family now, and I don't need her any longer."

Jordan propped his hands on Nathan's desk and leaned in. "All I'm asking is that you give her one more chance. If she blows it this time I swear I won't ever nag you about her again."

"Give me one good reason why I should."

"Because you're a good person, Nathan. Better than her, better than Dad. And I'll deny it if you repeat this, but at times even better than me. And though Mom will never admit it, not inviting her hurt her feelings, and you aren't the kind of guy who hurts people's feelings. And the guilt you're going to feel isn't worth the view from that moral high horse you're on."

"Wow." Nathan shook his head. "And here I thought you were just as shallow and self-absorbed as she is."

"It'll be our secret."

Nathan was quiet for a minute, then he blew out a breath and said, "All right, fine. One more chance. But if she blows it this time, that's it."

"Fair enough. Are you going to call and tell her?"

Nathan glared at him.

"Or I could do it," Jordan said. He hoped his mom came through this time, because he was tired of making excuses for her. In fact, if she let them down again, it might be enough to push him over the edge as well. And who knows, maybe it would snap some sense into her if both her sons shut her out.

"That reminds me, we haven't gotten your RSVP yet," Nathan said.

"It's on my to-do list. But you know I'll be there."

"I assume you'll be bringing a date."

"At least one. No more than three."

Nathan shot him a "get real" look.

"What? I'm in pretty high demand."

"So," Nathan said, leaning back in his chair. "Getting back to what you were saying earlier, since I'm the *better* man, I guess that means you don't plan to fight me for the CEO position."

Jordan laughed. "I've got to get back to work."

He turned and crossed the room, and as he was walking out the door his brother called after him, "You know, you're not as smart as you think you are."

Yes, he was.

There was nothing to fight over because the CEO spot was already his. Though no one had come right out and said it, Nathan's engagement to Ana Birch—whose father owned Birch Energy, their direct competitor—had killed his chances at the big chair. Even worse, Walter Birch was suspected of conspiring in the sabotage. Even if Jordan did back out, Nathan didn't have a shot in hell.

Emilio Suarez, who was also in the running, married a woman whose ex-husband was responsible for one of the largest Ponzi schemes in a decade, and had dragged her name through the mud with his own. Though the charges against her had been dropped, there were a lot of people who still held her partially responsible for the millions they lost. The CFO of a billion-dollar corporation did not marry a woman linked to financial fraud without serious repercussions.

On top of that, Jordan had played an important role in Western Oil's recent success. He firmly believed that happy workers were productive workers. He appreciated and respected each and every man in that refinery, and that respect was returned unconditionally. Since he took over as COO, productivity had jumped by nearly fifteen percent.

As far as he was concerned, he had the position in the bag. It was just a matter of waiting for the announcement to make it official.

When he got back to his office, Jane was studying something on her computer monitor.

"Any problems with using the system," he asked.

"I'm familiar with this operating system and most of the programs. What I don't know, I'll figure out."

"Great, because starting this afternoon I have a mountain of work that needs catching up."

"That's why I'm here."

Or so he was supposed to believe. He just hoped that while she dug into his personal life—or at least tried to— she also was competent enough to get some *real* work done. And after hours, when the work was finished, the fun would begin.

Sometime before lunch it started to rain, so instead of walking to the restaurant, the secretaries decided to order in and ate lunch together in the break room. It was a huge relief for Jane, as she began to doubt if she would have even been able to make it to the lobby in the torture devices they had the nerve to call shoes. And though Jordan left for lunch, and she could have spent that hour in his office trying to get into his email and files, she was glad that she'd taken the opportunity to get to know the other secretaries in the office. Not that she'd gleaned any new information, but she'd begun to build a base of trust that might come in handy later.

There was a sense of camaraderie between the women that was completely foreign to her. At Edwin Associates she worked mostly with men who barely gave her the time of day, and in her parents' practice…well, her siblings had to be the most competitive people on the planet. Sometimes she felt smothered under the weight of their enormous egos. Here, everyone seemed to like and respect one another. It was a nice change.

Jane returned to her desk at one, and Jordan walked in fifteen minutes later. After that, he didn't leave the office for the rest of the day, so she didn't get another chance to investigate. But she did make a good-size dent in that pile of work he'd warned her about. In fact, she was so engrossed in what she was doing, Jordan had to remind her at seven-thirty to leave.

"Sorry, I guess I lost track of time."

"No need to apologize," he said, leaning in his office doorway, tie loosened, looking slightly rumpled and attractive as hell. He was the sort of guy that no matter what he wore—be it a tailored suit or a pair of sweatpants and a T-shirt—he would make a girl's heart beat a little faster. "Most temps are out the door at five on the nose. If you're trying to impress me, it's working."

Honestly, she really had just lost track of time. When she got her head in the zone, the rest of the world ceased to exist, and hours passed like minutes. Besides, it wasn't as if she had anything to go home to.

"I can stay if you need me," she told him, realizing right after she said it how terribly pathetic it was that her social life was so barren, she would rather stay at work. She could tell herself that she simply wanted to stay until after he left, so she could have unlimited access to his office, but it would be a lie.

Even more pathetic was the disappointment she felt when he said, "Go home, Jane." Then it occurred to her that all day he had referred to her as Miss Monroe, and now he had used her first name. She'd never been too crazy about her name, but the way he said it, in that smooth-as-velvet voice, made her feel warm all over.

She shut down her computer, slipped her shoes back on, and stood. Following a full afternoon off her feet, they had stopped hurting, but she knew that by the time she made it to her car she would probably be in agony again.

"So," he said, as she got her coat and purse out of the closet. "How would you rate your first day?"

"Besides spilling coffee on my new boss, I'd say it was all right." She dropped her purse on the desk to put on her coat, but before she could, he took it from her and helped her into it. It was very gentlemanly of him, and she couldn't help wondering if he did it for his regular secretary.

"Thank you," she said, turning back to him and grabbing her purse. "I'll see you tomorrow."

"I'll walk you down."

To the lobby? "Oh...you don't have to—"

"I won't be out of here for a couple of hours. I could use a few minutes' break." He gestured to the open door. "After you."

For some reason the thought of being in the elevator alone with him so late in the evening gave her a serious case of the jitters. She wasn't used to being around men who were so blatantly sexy. Not to mention flirty. What if he came on to her? What would she do?

Of course he wouldn't come on to her. She barely knew him. Besides, if he were some sort of sexual deviant, she was sure she would have heard about it at lunch, but the other women had nothing but good things to say about him.

Jen had left for the night, and there was a different guard posted by the elevator. He was older than Michael but no less intimidating.

"Jane, this is George Henderson, the night guard. George, this is Miss Monroe. She'll be temping for me until Tiffany comes back from her maternity leave."

"Ma'am," George said, nodding stiffly, and he didn't even crack a smile.

Jordan hit the button for the elevator and it opened almost immediately. She stepped in first, leaning against the back wall to take some of the pressure off her feet because, surprise, they had already begun to throb again. Jordan settled beside her, his arm grazing the sleeve of her jacket. Did he have to stand so close?

As the doors slid closed she experienced the oddest sensation of anticipation, as if any second he was going to do something drastic, like...oh, yank her into his arms and kiss her senseless. And wow, wouldn't that be awful, because she was sure he was probably a terrible kisser.

She gave her head an exasperated shake. How he kissed was of no consequence to her, because she wouldn't be kissing him.

"Everything all right?" Jordan asked, and she realized he was watching her with a curious look.

She smiled. "Yes, fine."

"Something on your mind?"

She shook her head. "No."

"How are your feet?"

"Starting to hurt again."

"You might want to rethink the shoes tomorrow. Besides, I like you better when you're shorter."

She must have looked confused because he added with a grin, "I'm intimidated by tall women."

Somehow she doubted that. He struck her as the kind of man who wasn't intimidated by *anyone*.

"So, do you live close by?" he asked.

"Not too far. About fifteen minutes."

"Well, be careful driving. Even if the rain stopped it's cold, so it might be slick out there."

"I will."

The doors opened to the main lobby. She figured that would be it. He would say goodbye and ride back up, but he stepped out with her. He walked her all the way through the lobby, past the coffee shop, which was now closed, and past the guard station to the front door.

"Well, thanks for walking me down," she said, as he reached past her to open the door.

"I've come this far," he said with a shrug. "I may as well walk you to your car."

Five

He wanted to walk her all the way to her *car?* "But it's freezing out there and you don't have a coat," Jane said.

Jordan shrugged, as if it was no big deal. "I could use the fresh air."

Okay, this was getting a little weird. It was unlikely that he was worried about her safety, since the employee lot was monitored by security cameras. And even if that were the case, wouldn't he send a guard out with her instead? At Edwin Associates no one had ever bothered to open a door for her, much less escort her to her car. Was it possible that he suspected something, and he was going to spring it on her once they were out of the building? What if he knew she wasn't who she said she was?

Her pulse jumping, she stepped outside and he followed her into the chilly night. The wind had died down, but it felt as if the temperature had dropped. "I'm parked in the back."

"Lead the way," he said.

He walked beside her, and the farther from the building they went, the more nervous she began to feel. It must have shown, because after a minute he looked over at her and asked, "Is there a reason you're so edgy?"

"Is there a reason I should be?"

He grinned. "Because I'm walking you to your car?"

"Do you always walk your secretary out?"

"Would you be surprised if I said yes?"

"Would you be surprised if I were surprised?"

He laughed. "Do you always answer a question with a question?"

Only when she was nervous, and worried she would say the wrong thing. "Correct me if I'm wrong, but aren't you doing the same thing?"

"Touché. Maybe I think you're a really great secretary, and I'm worried you might slip in those behemoth heels and break a limb, in which case I would have to break in someone new."

"So what you're saying is, your motivation is purely selfish."

"Pretty much. My motto is, if there's nothing in it for me, what's the point?"

She couldn't tell if he was joking or serious.

As they approached her car she used her key fob to unlock it.

"Wow," he said, as they got closer and he saw the make. "That was not what I pictured you driving."

Her either. "It was a graduation present."

"College?"

"Yeah." Although actually it was law school. Her parents got a new car for each one of their kids when they passed the bar exam. Her oldest brother Richard got a fully restored muscle car, and for Will—the status monger—they bought a BMW. For her trendy sister, Mary, they purchased a cute and zippy red Miata, and for Jane, the "practical" child, they picked out a conservative, boxy white Volvo sedan.

Yeah, Mom and Dad.

He looked confused. "Did you actually request this? I mean, don't get me wrong, it's a really nice car…for a forty-something mother of two. I imagined you in something a little less…"

"Yeah." Her too. "It's not exactly my style, but it was a gift, so I'm sort of stuck with it." At least until she could afford something new. She'd taken a pretty hefty pay cut when she left her parents' firm and since then her savings had been slowly dwindling away.

She opened the driver's-side door and stood behind it, using it as barrier between them, not that she was afraid he was going to try something. Or maybe she was a little. Truthfully, she didn't know *what* to think. He was being so friendly and…flirty. She was definitely not the sort of woman whom people flirted with. And even if someone had, it probably would have had her retreating back into her shell.

He didn't need to know that.

She tossed her purse onto the passenger seat and clutched the top of the door to take some of the weight off her feet. "Well, I guess I'll see you tomorrow."

"You never did answer my question," he said.

"Which one?"

"Why are you so edgy?"

Oh, *that* one. She sort of hoped he'd forgotten about that. "Who says I am?"

He grinned and her knees went squishy again. Even with the door between them he was too close. He had a way of invading her space, even if he was standing five feet away.

"You're very good at that," he said.

"What?"

"Not answering questions."

As a lawyer, she'd had a lot of practice.

"And I know you are," he said.

"I am what?"

"Edgy." He leaned in a little closer, and—*Oh my God*—rested his hands on the top of the door beside hers, boxing them in, so that his thumbs were resting on her pinkies. She had to fight not to jerk away, and her heart started hammering about a million miles a second. She was alone, in the dark, in a deserted parking lot with a man she barely knew, her heart racing with a combination of fear and anticipation. And she *liked* it. What happened to practical, play-it-safe Plain Jane?

"You don't have to be afraid of me," he said, his face so close she could count the individual hairs on his chin. "I'm harmless."

Oh, she seriously doubted that.

"I'm not afraid," she said. More like *petrified*.

"Then why are you hiding behind your car door?"

Couldn't put anything past him, could she?

"Maybe I just don't like you," she said, hoping he didn't hear the quiver in her voice, or feel her hands trembling.

He shook his head. "Nah, that can't be it. I mean, look at me. I'm handsome, and rich."

"And modest."

He grinned. "Exactly. What's not to like?"

She had the feeling he wasn't nearly as arrogant and shallow as he wanted her to believe, that maybe it was some sort of…defense mechanism. And boy did she know about those. She had practically invented the concept. Keep a safe distance, don't let anyone too close, and no one could hurt her.

"Admit it," he said. "You like me."

She wasn't supposed to like him. Not like this. Not at *all*. But he was right, she did. And it seemed as though, the harder she pushed him away, the harder he pushed back.

"You're my boss," she said, but it came out all soft and breathy.

His eyes locked on hers. His pupils were dilated so wide his irises had all but disappeared. "Not after we walked out of the building."

She tried to look away but she was riveted. Then his thumbs brushed across the tops of her fingers, sending a ripple of sensation up her hands and into her arms. If the car door wasn't there between them she would…well, she wasn't sure what she would do. But she would definitely do something.

"I—I really need to get home," she said.

"You don't want to go home."

He was right. She didn't want to leave. She could stand there all night just looking into his eyes. Listening to the deep hum of his voice. Feeling the brush of his thumbs over her fingers. Back and forth. And then he was closer, and she realized he was leaning in. Oh my God, he was going to kiss her. He was actually going to kiss her, right there, in the parking lot. And she *wanted* him to. In that instant she didn't care about the investigation or her career.

She should have pushed him away, or run like hell, but instead she felt herself leaning in, her chin lifting, her eyes drifting closed. His face was so close she could feel the warmth of his breath against her lips and she held her own breath in anticipation…then she felt his breath shifting the hair over her ear and he whispered, "Yeah, you like me."

She felt him let go of the car door and by the time she

dragged her eyes open he was already walking away. She stood there, stunned and confused, wondering what the hell had just happened.

Whoa.

Jordan walked briskly back to the building, his pulse jumping, sweating despite the cold, wondering what the hell had just happened.

He hadn't meant to do more than tease Jane a little, yet he had come within a millimeter of pressing his lips to hers. He couldn't remember a time when the idea of doing nothing more that kissing a woman had gotten him so hot and bothered.

He shook his head and laughed in spite of himself. He was supposed to be toying with Jane, and here he was in even worse shape than her.

One thing was clear, though. The coy routine was no act. He could feel her unease as they rode the elevator down to the lobby, and when they got to the car. When he touched her hands, she was actually trembling. For the life of him he couldn't understand why a woman as beautiful and sexy as her could be nervous around anyone. She was a total contradiction. Confident and capable one minute, shy and awkward the next. If he didn't know any better he might have thought that he had two different women working for him. Or that this was some sort of twisted practical joke.

As he reached the building he heard Jane's car start, then pull out of the lot, but he resisted the urge to turn around and watch her drive away. Instead he pushed his way through the door and back into the lobby, asking the guard on duty, "Hey, Joe, you got a pen?"

"Sure thing, Mr. Everette." He grabbed a pen from his

station and handed it to him. "I take it it's going to be another late one."

"You know it." He jotted Jane's license plate number on the palm of his hand and handed the pen back. "Thanks."

He rode the elevator up to his office. He'd wondered all day if Jane Monroe was really her name, and he was about to find out.

He logged onto his computer and pulled up the website he'd registered for earlier that day—a service that accessed personal information through license plates. He punched in her number and the information popped up on the screen almost instantly.

Huh. Her name really was Jane Monroe. It listed her address, which he jotted down for future reference, and as she'd claimed, it was about fifteen minutes away. It also listed her birthday, which he was surprised to find was tomorrow.

Well, that had been almost too easy. He thought for sure they would have sent her in under an assumed name.

He pulled up a new page and logged onto a search engine, typing in her name. It came back with a couple hundred thousand hits. He scrolled the first couple of pages, finding an artist, a photographer, a professor at a university in Boston. There was even an actress who played bit parts on several popular television dramas. But no Jane Monroe investigator anywhere.

He started a new page but this time he typed in Jane Monroe, Texas. He got a hit for a website called *Linked Up,* a place to look up professional profiles. A Jane Monroe in El Paso, Texas, was the first on the list, but under profession it was listed as lawyer. That couldn't be right.

He typed in Jane Monroe, Lawyer, this time, and got a hit for a family-owned El Paso practice called Monroe Law Group. There was a small photo of the family on the info page. There was an older couple who were clearly the parents, two sons, and two daughters. One of the daughters had dark hair and was very attractive, but looked nothing like Jane. The other was borderline mousy with unremarkable brown hair worn in a long, straight style, wire-rimmed glasses that were a little too large for her face and a shapeless gray suit that made her look as though she was slouching. She wasn't unattractive, but compared to the rest of the family, she seemed to almost fade into the background. But there was something familiar about her. Something about the shape of her face, and the tilt of her mouth…

No way.

He looked closer, expanding the page to make the photo larger. Damn. Even bare he would recognize that plump bottom lip anywhere. The woman in the photo was *Jane*.

He sat back in his chair, shaking his head, having a tough time reconciling the image on his screen with the blonde beauty working as his secretary. And if she was an attorney in her family practice, what the hell was she doing working at Edwin Associates?

He checked the individual profiles, but hers was missing. Maybe she had left and they hadn't gotten around to changing the photo.

He tried a few more searches with different key words, but he'd reached a dead end. He could only assume that her career as a lawyer was an unremarkable one. Which might explain why she'd left it.

He blew out a frustrated breath. Honestly, he didn't even know why he cared. She was a toy to him. A way to amuse himself until she was finished here. Not to mention a way to take out his frustration against the people who should have trusted him. She was nothing to him, yet there was something about her that just…fascinated him. It was rare that any woman had that sort of effect on him, and frankly, he didn't like it.

Jordan went into his browser history and erased all evidence of his searches and any activity on the license plate site, then he erased the link for the site from his favorites, just in case. For all he knew Jane could be some sort of computer whiz and just waiting for the opportunity to get into his computer. And since he would be at the refinery most of tomorrow morning, she would certainly get her chance. He wasn't exactly thrilled with the idea of someone snooping around in his office, going through his things, but the sooner she found what she was looking for, or better yet, didn't find it, the sooner she would be out of his hair.

Walking into work the next morning after that almost-kiss in the parking lot was one of the hardest things Jane ever had to do. Though no one had seen what had happened, she couldn't shake the feeling that everyone would look at her and just *know*. And she could swear the guards posted at the security station snickered as she passed through.

She knew it was silly, and probably a figment of her imagination, but after a long sleepless night, she wasn't exactly functioning with all cylinders. And she was still no closer to understanding what had happened. Why he had come so close to kissing her then just…walked away. Was it some sort of game to him?

Of course it was. He was toying with her, pushing her buttons. The question was why? Because he could?

She joined the group of people waiting by the elevator then followed them inside when the doors opened, standing against the back wall. The spot where she'd stood last night with Jordan.

The worst part of last night was the realization that if he really *had* kissed her, she would have let him. She was not the kind of woman to let men she barely knew kiss her. Nor did she base her self-worth on looks, or the attention she got from the opposite sex. But when Jordan stroked her fingers and gazed into her eyes, she'd never felt so attractive, so *wanted* in her entire life. Or so confused and dejected when he turned away.

He'd made a complete fool of her, and she had made it all too easy. Her only consolation, upon arriving home and reading the file that had been faxed over from Edwin Associates, was learning that Jordan Everette hadn't always been the charming, handsome, confident man that he was now.

Though she would have pegged him for a jock, and probably class president, she couldn't have been more wrong. According to his file he used to be a scrawny, awkward, socially inept intellectual with an IQ in the genius range. He had graduated top of his class in prep school and attended an Ivy League college, where he not only grew several inches in height and took up weight lifting, he completed the business program a full year and a half early.

At the age of twenty-one he'd inherited a trust fund that he immediately invested and multiplied exponentially within only a few years. He could have lived in luxury and never lifted a finger for the rest of his life, but he chose instead to embark on a career with Western Oil, where he climbed the ranks with record speed. To meet him, one might suspect he'd made it where he was on personality and charm alone, but that wasn't the case at all. He'd worked damned hard.

The current CEO had plans to step down soon and if she believed what Jen told her at lunch yesterday, Jordan had a decent shot at his position. If he wasn't guilty of sabotage, that is.

The doors opened at the top floor and she stepped out. She showed her badge to Michael Weiss, who smiled and waved her past, and said hello to Jen on her way through the lobby.

"Aren't those just the cutest shoes!" she said, admiring Jane's peep-toe Dior pumps.

"Thanks." She didn't usually spend a week's pay on shoes, but they were really cute, and though the heel was a whopping four inches, they didn't pinch her toes. "Is Mr. Everette in yet?"

"Eight on the nose."

She forced a smile. "Great!"

"Oh, and happy birthday."

She blinked. "How did you know it's my birthday."

She smiled cryptically. "You'll see."

Adding curiosity to the nervous knots in her stomach, Jane walked down the hall. She had already decided that if Jordan—make that Mr. Everette—said anything about last night she was going to act like it was no big deal. She stepped into her office, jerking to a stop before she reached her desk. Sitting on the corner, with a mylar balloon stuck in the center, was an enormous arrangement of butter yellow roses. At least two dozen.

She dropped her purse in her chair and leaned down to inhale the delicate scent. There was no card, and nothing lying on her desk. Who in the world—

"I wasn't sure what kind to get," Jordan said from behind her and she whipped around.

He stood in his office doorway, and her heart dropped so hard and fast at the sight of him, it sucked the breath right out of her.

She had tried to convince herself last night that he wasn't

as amazingly handsome and devastatingly charming as she first thought, but he really was. And despite last night, if he were to walk up to her, take her in his arms and plant a kiss on her right then and there, she probably wouldn't do a damned thing to stop him.

Where was *Practical Jane* when she needed her?

"You did this?"

"Guilty."

If he was trying to butter her up, it was *so* working. "They're beautiful. How did you know it was my birthday?"

"I could tell you, but then I would have to kill you."

And he obviously *wasn't* going to tell her. "Well, thank you. They're lovely."

"Don't take your coat off," he said.

"Why not?"

"Because we're leaving."

Six

We? As in the two of them. *Together?*

"Um, where are we going?" Jane asked.

"To the refinery. I told you I would bring you along the next time I went."

She looked at the inbox on her desk, piled high with work that still needed catching up on. "But I have so much work—"

"It'll keep."

"But—"

"I'll go get my coat. The limo will be waiting."

He disappeared into his office. He clearly wasn't taking no for an answer. And the idea of being stuck in a car with him after last night made her knees go squishy.

He was back a minute later with his coat on. "Let's go."

Having no choice in the matter, she snagged her purse off the chair and followed him to the elevator.

"Can you take my calls?" he asked Jen as they passed

her desk. "I'm taking Jane on a tour of the refinery. We'll be back later this afternoon."

"Of course, Mr. Everette," she said.

Later this *afternoon?* How long would the tour take? And would she be spending the entire time with him?

Michael must have pressed the elevator button for them because the door opened as they were approaching. They stepped inside, and as the doors slid closed, her heart climbed up to lodge in her throat.

Would he stand too close again? Bring up what happened last night?

Thankfully his phone chose that moment to start ringing. He looked at the display and said apologetically, "I have to take this."

She breathed a quiet sigh of relief and silent thank-you for the caller's convenient timing. He talked during the entire ride down to the lobby and the walk to the limo that was waiting for them outside the front door. She got in first, sitting with her back to the driver, and he slid in across from her. He was still talking as the car pulled out of the lot and headed east.

She sat back and tried to relax, hating that she felt so awkward and inept around him. When she worked at her parents' practice her competence had never been in question. In fact, she usually felt as though she was butting her head against the ceiling, desperate to break from the confines of the position her parents kept her in. She knew she was damned good and she had wanted to prove it, but they were always holding her back. As an investigator she felt completely out of her element and was flying blind, but at least they were giving her a chance to prove herself.

She glanced at Jordan, thinking that she would kill to see a photo of what he'd looked like when he was still in his awkward, geeky phase. Probably not half as awkward and geeky as she had been. Despite being two years younger than her classmates she had been several inches taller than most of the other girls, and straight as a board from neck to knees, with no sense of fashion and a bad case of acne that weekly visits to a dermatologist couldn't even clear up. Not to mention a sister who took morbid satisfaction in reminding Jane on almost a daily basis just how pretty she *wasn't*. To say that she had self-esteem issues was a serious understatement.

She wondered what her life would have been like if instead of constantly tearing her down, her sister had tried to help her. If, when Jane complained to her mother that she wasn't as pretty as Mary, her mother had told her that she was pretty in her own way, instead of saying, "You have something better than beauty, Jane, you have brains."

If her own mother didn't think she was pretty, there was clearly no hope for her.

She looked out the window, watching the city pass by, feeling inexplicably sad. Maybe they were right. Maybe she was fooling herself into thinking anything had changed. Maybe the kind of pretty she had now, the kind that came from layers of overpriced cosmetics, didn't count anyway, because underneath it she was still the same Plain Jane. Maybe all she was doing was cheating the system.

"Penny for your thoughts."

She turned to find Jordan watching her. She was so lost in thought she hadn't even realized he was off the phone.

"It looks like it might rain again," she said.

"I've never known the threat of rain to make someone look so sad."

Did she really look that sad?

She shrugged. "I'm just ready for spring. I've never been much of a cold weather person."

"Do you have any special plans tonight?"

"Plans?"

"For your birthday."

Oh, that. "Not tonight. But I'm having dinner with my family on Friday."

"You have brothers and sisters?"

"Two brothers, one sister."

"Older or younger?"

Why the sudden interest in her family? And wasn't she supposed to be pumping *him* for information? "I'm the youngest."

He nodded sympathetically. "I know how that is."

"You just have the one brother?" she asked, even though she already knew the answer. But if she kept him talking, she might learn something valuable to the case.

"Just Nathan. Although why my mother had children at all is a mystery to me. She wasn't exactly maternal."

"Mine was Supermom. She had a full-time career and was home to help us with our schoolwork every night."

"There it is," he said, gesturing out the window as they approached the refinery.

She had driven by it hundreds of times but she'd never actually been there. The sheer size had always astounded her. With all its stacks and towers and maze of pipes and tubing that seemed to stretch for miles, it was a wonder they could make heads or tails of it. "So, you're in charge of all of this?"

He smiled and nodded. "Yep."

She could see that he took a tremendous amount of pride in that fact.

"But I don't do it alone. I have a stellar staff." He pointed to a building at the south end of the complex. "That's our research facility. We employ several of the leading scientists in the field of alternative fuel, and devote more money annually into biofuel development than any of our competitors. I'm particularly interested in the use of algae as an alternate energy source. We're even considering a company name change to reflect the changing industry."

She had no idea Western was so versatile. "It sounds as if you really love what you do."

"It's an exciting industry to be a part of right now."

"What made you get into the oil business?"

"My brother."

That was sort of sweet. "You wanted to follow in his footsteps?"

"Actually, I did it to piss him off."

She must have looked really surprised, because he laughed.

"Okay, that wasn't the only reason. I figured it would be a stepping stone to something bigger and better. Turns out I really liked it. And I'm damned good at it. So good that I'm going to be CEO."

"You sound pretty confident about that."

"That's because I am."

"It doesn't bother you, competing against your own brother?"

He locked his eyes on her, and something in his expression made her knees feel squishy. "I believe that when you want something, you should go after it, all pistons firing. Don't you agree?"

Normally a question like that, spoken with such a suggestive undertone, would have her scrambling back into her shell. Instead she heard herself say, "I guess it just depends on what you want."

A grin curled his lips, but before he could reply the limo came to a stop and the door opened. She breathed a sigh of relief, because with that single comment she had exhausted her arsenal of witty comebacks. This flirting business sure wasn't easy, but with a little practice she just might get the hang of it.

She had figured that while Jordan conducted his business there, he would assign someone to take her on a tour, but that wasn't the case. He took her on the tour himself. Not only was the refinery a fascinating and complicated operation, it was obvious that everyone—from the managers to the men on the line—liked and respected him, and the feeling was clearly mutual. Jordan greeted the workers warmly, shaking hands, addressing almost every one of them by name. And his vast knowledge of the inner workings of the plant completely blew her away. By the time they finished the tour she knew more about refining oil than she ever imagined possible. And after seeing Jordan there, interacting with the people, she simply could not imagine him willingly doing anything to cause damage or harm here.

"So, what did you think?" he asked when they were in the limo and on their way back to Western Oil headquarters.

"I actually had a really great time. I never imagined an oil refinery could be so interesting."

"There wasn't time today, but someday soon I'll take you to the research lab. That's where the real magic happens."

"Are you in charge of that too?"

"That's my brother's territory, but I love hanging out there. My second choice to majoring in business was science."

"What made you choose business?"

"There's more money in it. And I'm good at it." His cell phone rang and he pulled it out of his coat pocket. "Sorry, I have to take this."

She looked out the window while he talked, realizing,

after they got back into the heart of the city, the driver was taking them in the opposite direction of the corporate building. Either he was lost, or Jordan had a stop to make before they went back.

The limo pulled up in front of Café du Soleil, one of the priciest French restaurants in the city. He obviously had a lunch date. She imagined he would send her back to the building alone, then the limo would go back and get him when he was finished.

Jordan hung up his phone just as the attendant opened the door to let him out, but he didn't move. "Ladies first."

Confused, she said, "Excuse me?"

"Well, I suppose we could eat in the car, but it's much nicer inside."

Wait a minute. *She* was his lunch date?

"Earth to Jane."

"We're eating here? Together?"

His brows rose. "Are you embarrassed to be seen with me or something?"

"No!" she said, laughing at the utter ridiculousness of the question. What woman wouldn't want to be seen with a man like him? "Of course not, I just…"

"It's your birthday, and since you don't have plans for this evening, you get a nice lunch."

"That's really sweet of you, but you don't have to do that."

"I don't have to, but I want to."

And she wanted him to, too. But what if someone she knew was there, and her cover was blown? Not that this was a regular hangout for her. It was about two stars out of her price range. And other than the people at Edwin, no one knew where she was working.

"If you don't like French cuisine we could go somewhere else," he said.

She was being silly. Of course she wouldn't run into anyone she knew there. And she couldn't ask for a better opportunity to get to know him.

"Lunch here would be lovely. Thank you."

They got out of the limo and went inside, Jordan placing a hand on her back as they walked through the door.

"Mr. Everette," the pretty young hostess with an authentic-sounding accent said. "So nice to have you back."

She took their coats, handing them off to the other young woman standing nearby and said, "Right this way."

Jane glanced around as they walked through the restaurant, relieved when she didn't see anyone she knew. She did notice the appreciative looks women cast Jordan as he passed, though. Not that she blamed them. Had she been dining there, and he walked in, she would have looked at him exactly the same way.

The hostess seated them near the window and said, "James will be right with you."

She was barely gone ten seconds when James appeared at the table. He addressed Jordan by name, listed the specials, then took their beverage orders. Jane ordered a Perrier.

"Are you sure you wouldn't like a glass of wine?" Jordan said. "Or better yet, champagne, since it is your birthday."

"I shouldn't while I'm working."

He grinned. "I promise not to tell your boss."

She was about to decline, and had to remind herself that this was not about her "job" at Western Oil. This was about the investigation, and pumping Jordan for information. For that, she could be the type of woman who imbibed at lunch.

She smiled and said, "In that case, I'd love some."

He ordered an entire bottle and the waiter trotted off to fetch it.

"I take it you eat here often, Mr. Everette," she said.

"Often enough to know that the *boeuf bourguignon* is to die for."

She looked at the menu, which was written entirely in French. And since she couldn't read French, she set it aside and said, "Then I think I'll have that."

"I have an idea," he said. "How about, when we're not in the office, you call me Jordan?"

"Okay. Jordan." It was completely ridiculous, but using his first name seemed so...intimate. "Does Tiffany use your first name when you're not in the office?"

He grinned. "No. And in answer to your next question, no, I don't take her out to lunch either."

"That wasn't my next question."

"Well, I figure it was bound to spring up eventually."

James reappeared with their champagne and poured them each a glass, then he took their orders. When he was gone, Jordan held up his glass and said, "A toast, to your... twenty-third birthday?"

He definitely knew what to say to make a girl feel good. "Twenty-ninth," she said, lifting her glass.

"Get out. You don't look a day over twenty-five."

She clinked her glass against his and took a sip. Of course it was delicious.

Jordan took a sip, then set his glass back down. "So, what was your next question?"

She opened her mouth to answer him, glancing past him at the the man walking in her direction from the restrooms. Her breath caught and her heart dropped, and her first instinct was to slide out of her chair and hide under the table. This *could not* be happening.

Please don't let him see me, she begged silently, willing herself to be invisible.

"Jane?" Jordan said, his brow furrowed with concern. "Are you okay?"

The man passed by the table, glancing briefly at her, and she held her breath…then he did a double take and stopped in his tracks.

Her heart plummeted into the pit of her stomach.

"*Jane?* Is that you?"

Seven

Jane cursed silently, but pasted on what she hoped was a pleasant, yet slightly disinterested smile. "Oh, hello, Drake."

Her ex looked her up and down and laughed. "Oh my God, I hardly recognized you. You look... *Wow*. What happened to you?"

What he meant was, what happened to drab, Plain Jane at whom men never cast a second glance? Well, Drake wasn't exactly God's gift to women. He wasn't particularly tall, or well built, or even all that good-looking, and the hairline that had begun to recede in his early twenties was now a full-fledged bald spot.

She ignored his question and instead asked, "How have you been?"

"Great! I don't know if you heard, but Megan and I are engaged. We set a date for this spring."

"Oh, congratulations," she said, digging her acrylic nails into the meat of her palms. She knew she was better off without him, but the news still stung. She had been with him for five years, two of those living together, but they had never once talked marriage.

After only nine months with Megan they were already *engaged*?

Drake had always complained that Jane didn't love him enough, and that she put her career before him, and it was probably true. He was her first serious boyfriend, and she had just assumed that he was the best she was ever likely to do, which in hindsight wasn't fair to him or her. He needed someone who worshipped the ground he walked on. Someone he could lord over and take care of. A woman who didn't threaten his massive ego. Megan, who wasn't exactly blessed in the brains department, was the perfect mate for him.

Still, it had been humiliating to be dumped for a woman with the IQ of a pencil sharpener.

Drake shook his head and laughed. "I just can't get over this. I mean, look at you!"

He glanced over at Jordan, who was watching the exchange with a mildly amused expression. "I'm sorry, you must be Jane's…?"

"Jordan Everette," he said, accepting Drake's outstretched hand.

"Drake Cunningham," Drake said. "I'm with Cruz, Whitford and Taylor. Junior partner."

Jordan clearly felt no need to validate his own ego by stating his occupation or position. He only nodded politely.

"I went to school with Jane," Drake said and Jane cringed inwardly. *Please don't say it*—"U of T Law."

Jordan flicked a look of surprise her way. "Is that so?"

She cursed silently. Now there were going to be questions, like why a law graduate would settle for a job as a secretarial temp. *Thanks a bunch, Drake.*

Drake turned back to Jane. "I heard you left the family practice, but there was no word as to who picked you up."

And thank God for that. He could have just completely blown her cover. If he hadn't already. "Actually, I've been taking a break from law," she said, and left it at that. She didn't owe him an explanation anyway.

Drake nodded somberly. "I totally get it. The law is cutthroat. Some people just can't take the pressure."

She gnashed her teeth and resisted the urge to kick him in the shin. It had always chapped his ass that Jane had a higher GPA, and graduated with higher honors.

He had to be loving this.

"Well," he said, glancing at his watch, "I have a meeting. But it was good to see you again. And I guess I'll be seeing you at the reunion."

"Reunion?" Jordan asked.

"Once a year a group of us from our law school graduating class get together and have a party," Drake told him.

Jane suddenly felt sick to her stomach. "I didn't see your name on the RSVP list." It was the only reason she had signed up to attend.

"I was supposed to be abroad but I rearranged my schedule." His face softened and he touched her shoulder, giving it a squeeze. "Hey, if it's still too hard for you—"

"Of course not," she said, resisting the urge to bat his hand away. Feeling him touch her turned her stomach, but she refused to give him the satisfaction of thinking she cared one way or the other.

"Great, then I guess we'll see you there."

We. Of course it was too much to hope that he wouldn't be bringing his fiancée.

Giving her shoulder a condescending pat, he walked away, and she grabbed her champagne glass and downed it in one swallow.

"Please tell me you didn't date that guy," Jordan said.

"Um…"

His brow lifted. "*Seriously?* Not only is he an arrogant jerk, but in the looks department you are *way* out of his league."

That was the first time anyone had accused her of that. "We were together for five years."

He looked so disappointed in her. "At least you came to your senses."

"Actually, he dumped me for Megan. About nine months ago."

"Tell me you're over him. Because you can do better, trust me."

"Of course I'm over him. He was never the love of my life. I'm just…I guess I'm still a little…bitter. And betrayed, since I'm the one who introduced him to Megan."

"She's a lawyer?"

"A dog groomer."

His brow popped up again.

"We owned a bichon frise and we took him to her for grooming. When Drake dumped me, my new apartment wouldn't allow pets, so she got my boyfriend *and* my dog."

"With the exception of the dog, I'd say you got the better end of the deal."

He was right of course. She never would have been happy married to Drake, even if he had asked. Her family thought he was the perfect man for her, which in retrospect should have been her first clue that the relationship would end in disaster. She should have taken it as a sign to run screaming in the opposite direction.

"So, you're a law graduate," Jordan said.

There was no denying it now. "My parents and my siblings, they're all lawyers, so it was just assumed I would be too."

"Let me guess, they're not too thrilled that you've abandoned the law."

"Actually, they don't know that I have. I lied and told them I've been working in the corporate law department of Andersen Technologies, a small corporation in El Paso. It's just easier that way."

The waiter appeared, depositing their salads at the table and refilling her glass.

She took a generous swallow. She should be thankful, that could have gone a lot worse.

Then why did she feel so lousy?

"So when is this reunion?" he asked.

"Next month. But I'm not going."

"Why not?"

"I can just see it," she said, breaking her roll and slathering butter on one half, even though she had pretty much lost her appetite the instant Drake appeared. "Me still single and alone while Drake struts around with his new fiancée on his arm. I don't think so. It would be too humiliating."

"So don't go alone."

"That's a great idea. The problem is, I'm not dating anyone right now."

"So take a friend."

"The thing about ending a long-term relationship is that friends pick sides, and since most of them were Drake's to begin with, I lost those in the split too."

He shrugged and said, "In that case, take me."

Eyes wide, Jane dropped her roll into her salad. Jordan stifled a grin as she swiftly fished it back out. "Take *you?*"

"Why not?" Jordan said. "I like parties."

She set her roll down and wiped her hand on her napkin. "Look, I appreciate the gesture, but I can't ask you to do that."

"You're not asking, I offered."

She shook her head. "I can't."

"Jane, that guy takes way too much pleasure from the fact that he thinks you're all alone pining for him. He needs a reality check."

"But that *is* reality. Except for the pining part. I *am* alone. And taking my boss to a party—"

"So I won't be your boss."

"But you *are* my boss."

"No one else needs to know that."

She nervously licked her lips. "What am I supposed to say? You're my...boyfriend?"

Her discomfort made him smile. She seriously had no clue how attractive she was. "Boyfriend, *lover*...whatever."

"But it would be a lie."

She didn't seem to have a problem with lying to him on a daily basis, and lying to her family about where she worked.

"Then you don't have to tell anyone anything." He slid his hand across the table and slipped his fingers around hers. They were ice cold, so he flashed her a smile that was sure to warm her from the inside out. "Besides, actions speak louder than words."

Her lips parted with a soft gasp and she tugged her hand free, eyes darting nervously to the people at the next table. "No. He would never buy that someone like you would date someone like me."

He sat back in his seat. "Why not?"

"Because..." She frowned and shook her head. "Never mind. I just...I think it would be a bad idea. I'm better off not going."

"Then he wins."

"So he wins, so what? It's not a competition. I don't care what he thinks any longer."

Another lie. For reasons that totally escaped him, she did care, which was why he'd offered in the first place. He saw the way she'd paled when Drake approached the table—although that could have had more to do with her fear of blowing her cover. But the pain in her eyes when he announced his engagement, that was real.

Rather than hide behind her morals—and her obvious insecurities—she needed to confront the situation. Confront Drake and Megan. Until she did, she would have a tough time moving on. Not that he had much experience with long-term romantic relationships. He'd never been with the same woman for five months, much less five years. Hell, five weeks was pushing the envelope. But he did know an awful lot about being let down by people he thought he could depend on.

And if that wasn't reason enough, he was pissed that the jerk had ruined her birthday lunch. And even worse, after five years together, he hadn't even remembered to wish her a happy birthday.

He wanted to push the issue, but he had the feeling that once Jane made up her mind, it would be hard to change it, so he let it drop. For now. Instead he tried to engage her in another round of witty banter, to lighten the mood, but she wasn't biting, and she only picked at her food. That guy had really done a number on her.

Honestly, he shouldn't have even cared. The problem was, he liked Jane. The fact that she genuinely seemed to have no clue how attractive she was fascinated him. And though he'd brought her here to screw with her, it didn't seem right to kick her while she was down. Besides, hurting her was never his intention. Hell, maybe he could help her.

There was definite chemistry there. Maybe what she needed was someone to pay attention to her, to make her see how beautiful and desirable she really was. To make her feel special. And while sleeping with her would of course be his ultimate goal, wherever this thing between them went, he would make certain that it was mutually beneficial.

The sort of woman he usually dated knew what she wanted, and wasn't shy about going after it. And what they usually wanted was his money, but since he had no intention whatsoever of getting tied down, that had never been a problem. Right about the time he began to get bored, they realized that they were wasting their efforts and the relationship fizzled out. No harm, no foul.

It might be an interesting change if, for once, he was the one doing the pursuing. And he was willing to bet, if she would give up what had most likely been a reasonably lucrative career as an attorney, for what he guessed was an entry-level position at an investigation firm, she wasn't hung up on status and wealth. Not to mention that she needed someone to show her that she could do better than that arrogant creep she had wasted five years with.

The more he thought about it, the more he liked the idea. Yes, she had been lying to him since the minute she met him, but that was her job, so technically there was no malicious intent. Besides, he wasn't exactly being honest either.

Jane was quiet on the ride back to the office, and other than thanking him for the tour and for lunch, didn't say more than a few words for the rest of the afternoon. She knocked on his office door at six to tell him she was leaving for the night.

"Is there anything you need before I go?" she asked. She just looked so…depressed.

"You know, he isn't worth it," Jordan said.

"I know. The truth is, I don't even know why I'm upset.

I didn't want to marry him. I don't even think I loved him."
She shrugged. "Maybe I'm just a sore loser."

"Try not to let it ruin your night. Call a friend. Go out
for drinks. Do something fun. It's your birthday."

She smiled, but it didn't quite reach her eyes. "I definitely will."

She was lying.

"Well, thanks again for the tour, and for the lunch."

"It was my pleasure."

"I'll see you tomorrow."

"See you tomorrow."

He had half a mind to walk her back down to her car,
but his cell rang. Since it was his mother, he was inclined
to let it go to voice mail, but he answered it. "Hey Mom,
what's up?"

"Well, did you talk to him?" his mother demanded.

Her brusque greeting didn't phase him. She always did
like to get right to the point. "Talk to whom?"

"Your brother."

Confused, he asked, "About what?"

"The invitation. To Nathan's graduation."

"You mean the wedding?"

"That's what I said," she snapped.

He saw no point in arguing with her. "You know I did.
I called you yesterday to tell you that he's inviting you.
Don't you remember?"

She was quiet for several seconds then said, "No, I'm
sure I would have remembered. I've been home all day."

He wasn't sure why her being home today had any
bearing on a call he made yesterday. "Well, I did."

"So, is he inviting me?"

Hadn't he just said he was? "Mom, are you okay?"

"I jush wish you would ansher me!" she slurred.

No wonder she wasn't making any sense; she was

hammered. He wondered if things had gone south with her latest man-friend, the filthy rich baron. Was she wallowing in self-pity?

"Yes, Mom, Nathan is inviting you. As I told you yesterday, you'll be getting an invitation any day. Probably tomorrow."

"And Mark will be there?"

Mark? "You mean Max? Nathan's son?"

"That's what I shed."

He sighed. There was no point continuing a conversation she wouldn't even remember in the morning. "Mom, I have to go. I'll call you tomorrow, okay?"

She mumbled something incoherent then hung up. He shook his head and dropped his phone on his desk. That was weird. His mother drank socially, but he'd never known her to get good and sauced. First time for everything, he supposed.

He turned back to his computer and tried to concentrate on his work, but his thoughts kept drifting back to Jane. If he knew women—and he liked to believe that he did—she was probably sitting home alone, with a gallon of chocolate ice cream and a spoon, watching a chick flick and having a pity party.

Well, that wasn't his problem. He couldn't force her to have a good time. Of course, if he hadn't insisted that they go to lunch, she wouldn't have seen her ex and she might actually be enjoying her birthday. So in essence, it was his fault.

He cursed and tossed down his pen. She was miserable and he was to blame, so of course there was only one thing he could do.

Make it right.

Eight

Jane wasn't expecting anyone to stop by, so she was surprised when, at seven-thirty, someone knocked on her door. She dropped the spoon into the ice cream container, set it on the coffee table and paused the movie she'd been watching. It was probably one of her siblings stopping by to say happy birthday. And while normally it annoyed her when they stopped by unannounced, she could use a bit of cheering up tonight.

Clad in a U of T sweatshirt, fleece pajama bottoms and fuzzy slippers, she shuffled to the door and pulled it open—and for an instant she thought her eyes must be playing tricks on her. Or maybe she'd fallen asleep on the couch and she was only dreaming that Jordan was standing in the hall outside her apartment door.

He was still dressed in his work clothes, and carrying a small square bakery box. It never ceased to amaze her how truly beautiful he was, although for the life of her she couldn't imagine what he was doing here.

He took in her shabby clothes, his gaze settling on her feet, and said, "Nice slippers."

Thank goodness she hadn't washed off her makeup yet. He probably would have taken one look at her, turned and run. "I wasn't expecting company."

"Despite promising me that you would go out and have fun, I kept having this mental picture of you sacked out in front of the television watching a chick flick, drowning your sorrows in a gallon of chocolate ice cream."

And he cared enough to stop by and make sure she was okay? First the tour, then lunch, now a visit to her apartment? Maybe she *was* dreaming.

"Am I right?" he asked.

Not exactly, but freakishly close. "It's a pint of caramel nut swirl and I wouldn't exactly call *The Terminator* a chick flick."

"The point is, you're here, and not out celebrating."

Yeah, and how did he even know where "here" was? Probably the same way he knew it was her birthday. The HR office had all of her personal information.

"You know," he said. "I dropped everything to race over here and save you from an evening of self-pity. The least you could do is invite me in."

Right, that would be the polite thing to do, even though the idea of Jordan in her apartment made her pulse skip.

"Sorry, of course." She pulled the door open and stepped out of the way, doing a quick mental inventory of her living room and kitchen, but any incriminating evidence was on her desk in the spare bedroom. There was nothing else in the apartment linking her to Edwin Associates. Not even in her bedroom. Not that he would be going in there. "Please, come in."

He stepped into her living room, and she closed the door behind him. He handed her the box. "This is for you."

"Oh, thank you."

Jordan took off his coat and hung it on the coat tree by the door. Then he did the same with his suit jacket. She stood watching, unsure of what to say or do. The whole point of the investigation was to catch his interest, and clearly she had. Now she didn't have a clue what to do about it, how to take control of the situation. He was too much man for a woman like her.

He loosened his tie, undid the top button on his shirt and rolled the sleeves to his elbows. He was making himself right at home, and she was a jumble of nerves. Her apartment wasn't what anyone would consider spacious, but with him there it felt downright tiny.

He nodded to the box that she was still clutching. "Aren't you going to open it?"

Of course, where were her manners? She slid the top open, and inside was a mini cake. "A birthday cake?"

"I figured you probably didn't have one, and everyone should have a cake on their birthday."

That was the sweetest thing anyone had done for her in a very long time. She hadn't heard word one from her own family—the people who were *supposed* to care about her—and this man who she barely knew had gone above and beyond to make the day special. "Thank you, Jordan."

"I'll bet that would go really well with a cup of coffee."

A cup of coffee was the least she could do. "Is French pressed coffee okay?"

"Of course."

She carried the box to the kitchen and set it on the counter, then she put the kettle on to boil and got out the coffee press and beans.

"Did you just move in here?" Jordan asked, gazing around her sparsely decorated living room.

"Nine months ago. I just haven't gotten around to doing much with it. I sold most of my furniture when I moved in with Drake, so I didn't have much of my own stuff when I moved out." She measured out the beans and set the grinder on Coarse, and when it was finished poured the ground coffee into the press. When the water started boiling she poured it in and set the timer on the oven for four minutes.

"This is good," he said.

She turned to find him leaning in the kitchen doorway eating what was left of her caramel swirl ice cream.

"It's my favorite," she said.

He took another bite and licked the spoon. "I hope you don't mind sharing."

"I have three more pints in the freezer." He could eat her ice cream anytime. And watching him, the way his tongue swept over the spoon, was giving her a hot flash, so she busied herself cutting them each a slice of cake.

"So, have you thought anymore about the reunion?" he asked.

"I haven't changed my mind, if that's what you mean." The timer beeped and she pulled two cups down from the cupboard.

"It doesn't seem fair that you should have to miss it just because your ex is there."

"Maybe I'll go next year." She pressed the plunger down then poured the coffee, adding a dash of creamer to his and leaving hers black. Picking up both cups, she swiveled around to hand him one, unaware that he was standing right behind her. She stopped so abruptly that the coffee sloshed over the brim of both cups and landed—of course—on him.

"Oh my God, I am *so* sorry."

He looked down at the stain spreading across the front of his shirt. "I'm beginning to think you're doing this on purpose."

She set the cups down and grabbed the towel hanging from the oven door handle. She ran it under the faucet, wrung out the excess water, and handed it to him. At least this time she hadn't lobbed an entire cup at him. "I didn't know you were right behind me."

"Don't worry about it." He dabbed at the stain, but it was already setting in. That was another of his shirts she had probably ruined. A few more days with her and he was going to need a new wardrobe.

"Maybe if we throw it in the washing machine right now it won't stain," she said.

His mouth tilted into one of those adorable grins. "You know, if you wanted to get me out of my clothes, all you had to do was ask."

Did he really think she was trying to get him naked? "I wasn't… I didn't mean—"

"Jane, I'm *kidding*." He tossed the towel onto the counter. "I came here to cheer you up and instead you're a nervous wreck."

He was right. He had been nothing but nice to her, and she was a bundle of nerves. What did she think he was going to do? Attack her? Why couldn't she relax when she was with him?

"I'm sorry," she said, feeling like a complete dope.

"Maybe I should just go."

"No!" She said it so forcefully he flinched. Was there no end to her making a complete ass of herself? She took a deep breath. "Of course you can go if you want to, but you don't have to."

"What is it about me that makes you so edgy?"

"I don't know. I guess I just suck at this."

"At what?"

"This…this…" she gestured absently "…flirting thing. That is what we're doing, right? I mean, I'm not imagining things, am I?"

That made him smile. "You're not imagining anything. And for the record, you're damned good at the flirting thing. When you're not acting like you're afraid of me."

"I'm sorry." There was no point in trying to pretend she was a sexy temptress when clearly she wasn't fooling anyone. "I just…I'm not used to being around men like you."

"Jane, you were around me all day and you were fine."

"Yes, but there were other people around."

"So, being *alone* with me makes you nervous."

She nodded.

"Because we have chemistry?"

"You're my boss."

"I told you last night, not after we leave work."

No, but he was still the subject of the investigation, and already she was having a tough time remaining impartial. "I could lose my job."

"I won't let that happen."

Maybe the makeover had been a bad idea. Of course, then he wouldn't have noticed her at all. Maybe the truth was, she wasn't cut out to be an undercover investigator. She wasn't cunning and clever. And she wasn't a manipulator. She wasn't even a very good liar. This was just too hard.

"Jane, do you like me?"

Why did he have to make this so difficult? "Yes, I like you, but—"

"And I like you too."

She almost asked him why. Why would someone like him like someone like her? Was it because of what he saw on the outside? Because she obviously didn't have the insides to match. "You barely know me."

"Is it too much to ask for the chance to *get* to know you?"

She chewed her lip, unsure of what to do, how to move forward. Though it defied logic, for some reason he seemed to be interested in her. There had to be a way to use that to her advantage. Could she use her ineptitude as a tool to string him along, to keep things from moving too quickly? To keep herself from getting into a situation that crossed the lines of morality?

It might actually work.

"Okay," she said.

He narrowed his eyes as if he didn't quite believe her. "Are you *sure?*"

"Yes, but under one condition. No one can know. When we're at work, I'm your secretary, nothing more. And that goes for the parking lot as well."

"Fine, but I have a condition too. You have to stop being afraid of me."

It's not as if she could shut it off like a switch. "I'll try."

"Maybe it would help if we break the ice."

"Break it how?"

"I think I should kiss you."

He thought *that* was going to make her less nervous? Just the idea had her heart racing. Not only because the thought of kissing him thrilled her, but she wasn't *supposed* to be kissing him. "Jordan—"

"Just one little kiss. It'll work. Trust me." He held out his hands. "Come here."

She looked at them nervously.

"I'm not going to bite," he said, then added with a grin, "unless you want me to."

At her wary look, he said, "Sorry, no more joking around." He wiggled his fingers. "Come here."

She really shouldn't be doing this, but honestly, what was the harm in one little kiss? Maybe it would eliminate that element of uncertainty. Besides, who would know?

She took a deep breath. *Okay, here we go. You can do this.*

She stepped toward him and took his hands, aware that hers were trembling. He held them loosely, very nonthreateningly. Without her high heels she was considerably shorter than him. At least six inches. She found herself focusing on the loosened knot of his tie.

"Jane, look at me."

She raised her eyes to his and just like last night in the parking lot, she was riveted. His irises were clear and bright; a mottled collage of brown and green flecks that were light at the outer edges, but grew darker and more intense as they reached the pupil. His eyes were just as extraordinary as the rest of him, and she couldn't stop herself from wondering again, what was he doing *here?* With *her?* Wasn't there an heiress or a supermodel he'd rather be kissing?

He tugged gently on her hands, drawing her closer. Her heart was beating so fast and hard it was becoming difficult to breathe. She hoped she didn't make an even bigger fool out of herself by dropping in a dead faint.

He lowered his head, leaning in, and she lifted her chin to meet him halfway, her eyes drifting closed. Then his lips brushed across hers.

Holy cow, she was kissing Jordan Everette. Or, he was kissing her. And it was...*perfect.*

If a soft peck felt this nice, she could just imagine how

a real kiss would feel. But she didn't want to imagine, she wanted to *know*.

He was right about one thing, she was feeling a whole mess of emotions right now, but the one she didn't feel was nervous.

He pulled back and looked down at her, searching her face, his voice a little rough when he said, "I know we agreed to one kiss, but you still look a little edgy to me."

One kiss, two. Who was counting, anyway?

He let go of her hands and reached up to cup her face in his palms, and the thrill of feeling him touch her made her knees go weak. This time when he kissed her, it wasn't a peck. This was deeper and hotter.

It wasn't as if she had never been kissed before, but she had never been kissed quite like this.

In what she considered a bold and daring move for someone like her, she reached up and laid her hands on his chest, feeling hard muscle and heat beneath his shirt. And he must have liked it because he made a gravelly sound in his throat. Then one of his hands dropped down to settle on her lower back, easing her in a little bit closer, against all that warmth and sinew. Probably too close, but at the same time not close enough.

One of his hands slipped under her sweatshirt, his palm settling against her bare skin, and in the same instant her leg buzzed where it was pressed against his thigh, as if he had a bee in his pants. She gasped with surprise at the unusual sensation and Jordan jerked his hand from beneath her shirt.

"Sorry. I'm supposed to be kissing you, not copping a feel."

"It's not that. Your leg is buzzing. It just startled me."

"It's my phone." He pulled it out of his pants pocket and

set it on the counter. "I have it on vibrate but it's rung four times since I've been here."

"Maybe you should answer it. It could be important."

"Being here with you is important too."

How was it that he always managed to say exactly the right thing? And as much as she wanted to keep kissing him, it was probably better that they take a break.

She stepped back, out of his reach. "You should at least look and see who it is."

He sighed and grabbed the phone from the counter, frowning as he thumbed through his recent calls. "There are three calls from Nathan, and two from Memorial Hospital."

"Call your brother, Jordan."

This time he didn't argue.

He dialed his phone and his brother must have answered on the first ring. "Why am I getting calls from Memorial Hospital?" Jordan asked him.

He listened for a minute, and she could tell by his deepening frown that something was wrong. Calls from hospitals were rarely ever favorable.

"But she's only fifty-four," he said. "Isn't she too young for that?" He listened for another minute, then said, "We can talk about it when I get there. I'm leaving right now."

He hung up his phone looking confused and a bit shell-shocked. "My mother had a stroke."

She gasped softly. "Is she okay?"

"They're not sure the extent of it yet, but they said she's not in any imminent danger. They have to run more tests."

Jane's maternal grandfather died from a massive stroke, so she knew from experience that it could be much worse. "Is there anything I can do?"

"I have the feeling this is going to be a long night, so I

probably won't be at work tomorrow. You'll have to hold down the fort."

"I can do that."

"I hate to bail on you, but I have to get to the hospital."

She touched his arm. "Of course. You should be with your family."

She followed him to the door where he put on his suit jacket, then his coat. "I'll call you tomorrow."

"If there's anything you need, just say the word."

"How about dinner Friday night?"

"I have dinner with my family Friday. But I'm free Saturday."

"You pick the place," he said, then he leaned down and kissed her, a soft brush of his lips that left her weak all over. "I'll see you later."

When he was gone, she closed the door, leaned against it and sighed. Oh, man, she was in trouble. If his phone hadn't rung, she could just imagine what they would be doing right now. And it would have nothing to do with drinking coffee and eating cake.

She wasn't supposed to like Jordan, but she did. Way too much for her own good. At least she was smart enough to realize that it wouldn't last. She was just a passing phase. She had to keep that in mind when he was kissing her, and touching her.

She couldn't deny that she was attracted to him, and being around him was a bit of a thrill, but it wouldn't last. If she wanted to come through this with her career intact, she needed to keep her perspective.

Next time they were alone, she wouldn't be giving in quite so easily.

Nine

Jordan didn't appreciate the severity of his mother's condition until he walked into her hospital room twenty minutes later. For some reason he expected her to be sitting up, her usual primped self, demanding and difficult and making a general nuisance of herself. He figured it was some sort of volley for attention. To see her lying in bed, pale and weak and hooked to a maze of tubes and wires was a shock. And though he had never seen her so much as flinch in the face of adversity, she was scared.

Nathan sat in a chair across the room. He stood when Jordan came in.

"Hey, Mom," Jordan said, walking to her bedside and taking her hand. She squeezed his weakly. "How are you feeling?"

She blinked rapidly and patted her throat.

"She can't talk," Nathan said.

He was about to ask why, but a nurse walked in.

"Time to change your IV, Ms. Everette," she said cheerfully.

Nathan nodded his head toward the door. Jordan tried to let go of his mother's hand to follow him, but she tightened her grip, looking panicked.

"Mom, I need to talk to Nathan for a minute. I promise I'll be right back."

She reluctantly let go of his hand. He followed his brother out into the hall. "She looks bad, Nathan."

"I know. But the doctor assured me that she's stable."

"Why can't she talk?"

"They think the stroke affected the speech center of her brain. She also has some weakness on her left side."

"But it's not permanent."

"He said that with physical therapy the weakness will improve, but she'll probably never be able to talk normally, even with speech therapy."

For a woman so hung up on appearances, that was going to be difficult for her to accept. "How did this happen? Isn't she too young?"

"Apparently not. The doctor did say that it would have been a lot worse if she'd waited any longer to come in."

"How did she get here?"

"A gentleman friend. I guess she called him and she wasn't making any sense. He suspected something was wrong and called 911."

Jordan's heart bottomed out. He leaned against the wall beside the door, shaking his head at the depth of his stupidity. "Son of a bitch."

"What?"

"She called me too. She was slurring her words and asking about things we already talked about. I thought she was drunk. I should have realized something was really wrong."

"Jordan, there's no way you could have known. Like you said, she's not that old. A stroke was the last thing we would have expected. If she had called me I probably would have assumed the same thing."

But she hadn't. She'd called him. She'd needed his help and he had completely failed her. If she hadn't called her "man friend" who knows how much worse off she could be? She could have *died*.

"I should have at least gone and checked on her," he said.

"You know that if it were one of us with a problem, she probably wouldn't even be bothered to show up at the hospital."

That didn't make him feel any less guilty. If he had realized there was a problem and called 911 immediately, maybe the damage would have been less severe.

When they walked back into the room she was waiting anxiously. After that, any time he and Nathan even got close to the door she would get a panicked look, but when she tried to speak, the words came out garbled and slurred.

She drifted in and out of sleep all night while the brothers took turns sitting at her bedside. Nathan had called their father as a courtesy, even though he and their mother hadn't spoken a civilized word in years, so both Nathan and Jordan were shocked when he came to visit Wednesday afternoon. Even more shocking was that she looked happy to see him.

It gave Jordan and his brother a chance to sneak off to the cafeteria to grab a cup of coffee and a bite to eat.

"She's not going to be able to stay by herself for at least a couple of weeks," Nathan said. "Maybe even longer. We'll have to hire a full-time nurse. And both speech and physical therapists."

"Or she could stay with you," Jordan said, grinning at the look his brother shot him.

"I would never do that to Ana. Although, the fact that she can't talk will make her a lot less annoying."

"That's a horrible thing to say," Jordan said, but he was trying not to smile.

"It's pretty ironic, don't you think? She couldn't be bothered to be there for us, but we're expected to take care of her."

"She's really scared. I've never seen her like this. It's hard not to feel sorry for her."

"I give her a month before she's back to her demanding and manipulative old self."

Jordan wasn't so sure about that. Maybe this would be a wake-up call for her. A chance to become a decent mother—a decent human being—before it was too late. Or maybe he was just fooling himself.

"I sure was surprised when Dad showed up," Nathan said. "Or maybe it isn't such a surprise, all things considered."

"What do you mean?"

"I think he still loves her."

"Still? I didn't know he ever did. I thought they had to get married because she was pregnant."

"I thought so too, but Dad says no. He told me, and I quote, 'He loved her more than life itself, and all she wanted from him was his name and as much of his money as she could get her greedy hands on.'"

"I guess that explains why he was always so unhappy."

"He told me that he was bitter and heartbroken and instead of taking it out on the person who deserved it, he took it out on us. The same way Grandma Everette took it out on him."

Jordan laughed. "Get out. Frail little Grandma Everette used to knock Dad around?"

"That's what he said. And she probably wasn't so frail back then."

Damn. It was tough to imagine their father letting anyone push him around. And Jordan had just assumed that their parents hated each other. He never understood why they had stayed together for twenty years. Maybe their father had held on to the hope that she would grow to love him. Clearly that had never happened.

When they finished their lunch and got back to their mother's room their dad was still there. He was sitting on the edge of the bed holding her hand. As far as Jordan could recall it was the first time he'd ever seen them touch.

He just hoped she wasn't afraid and clinging to the past. He hoped she wasn't using their father, and as soon as she was well would cast him aside yet again. He hoped, but given her behavior since…well, as long as Jordan could recall, the odds weren't very good.

Though she felt more than a little devious for taking advantage of the situation, Jordan's absence had given Jane unlimited access to his office for two days. She had to keep reminding herself that it was her job, and really, she was doing him a favor. If she wasn't able to prove he was guilty, that could only mean that he was innocent. His career would be safe, and he would be none the wiser.

That was what she hoped anyway.

She searched through his files but there was nothing incriminating, so, using the jump drive, she downloaded his emails—which weren't password protected—and spend most of the afternoon at her computer reading them. She also uploaded a spyware program that would make it possible for the tech guys at Edwin Associates to monitor any future emails.

Most of his current emails were of a professional nature, and the handful that were personal had nothing to do with the sabotage, nor were they the least bit suspicious. What she needed to see were his personal financial files, but he obviously didn't keep those at work, meaning she needed to get on to his personal computer at home. When she reported her findings, or lack thereof, to her superiors, they reached the same conclusion. She was to continue to monitor his phone calls and take the steps necessary to infiltrate his home. She also wanted to get a look at his incoming and outgoing calls on his cell phone. Until there were grounds for a warrant, they couldn't get a hold of the call records from his provider.

Her bosses seemed pleased, and maybe a little surprised, to learn that Mr. Everette was actually pursuing her, and if they were concerned about her crossing any lines, they didn't mention it. If it meant getting the information they needed, maybe they would forgive a few minor transgressions. The question was, could she? Could she sell herself out that way?

Between the investigation and her regular duties, Jane was swamped, so she stayed late Thursday to keep on top of things. She didn't get home until after ten. She grabbed her mail on her way into the building and rifled through it as she walked up the stairs to the second floor—her Visa bill, a few pieces of junk and something that looked like a wedding invitation. Curious, she started to rip it open as she walked down the hall to her apartment.

"I was beginning to think you weren't coming home," someone said. She squeaked with surprise, stumbling to a stop and dropping the mail.

Jordan grinned up at her from where he sat on the floor outside her apartment door. "Late night at work?"

Her heart lifted at the sight of him, then took a sharp dive. "Did something happen? Is your mom okay?"

"She's fine," he said as he pushed himself to his feet. He was dressed in black slacks and a black leather jacket. "In fact, they're cutting her loose tomorrow."

She crouched down to collect her mail. "What are you doing here?"

He shrugged, looking physically and emotionally drained. "All I know is, I was on my way home from the hospital to get some sleep, and somehow I ended up here. I guess I just wanted to see you."

She didn't even know what to say. Of all the people he could have gone to, he chose her?

"I know I shouldn't keep dropping in on you un-announced."

"No, it's okay." She walked past him to unlock the door.

"I can leave if it's a bad time."

She pushed the door open and switched on the light. "It's not a bad time. Come in."

He walked inside, and she stepped in behind him, closing and locking the door. She turned to tell him to take off his jacket, but before she could get the words out his arms were around her, pulling her close, hugging her fiercely. She dropped her purse and wrapped her arms around him, hugging him just as hard.

He buried his face against the side of her neck, his breath warm on her skin. "You cannot even imagine how long and stressful the past two days have been."

"Do you want to talk about it?"

"Right now, I think I'd just like to hold you."

That was okay too.

Since it was what he seemed to need, she held him close,

rubbing his back, until she could feel the tension begin to leak out of him. Seeing this vulnerable side of him, knowing that he even had one, changed her perception of him somehow. Yes, he was rich and powerful and gorgeous, but underneath it all, he was just a man. An extraordinary one, unquestionably, but nothing to feel threatened or intimidated by. In fact, it was a kind of a turn-on.

"Have I ever told you how good you smell?" he asked.

Something in his voice, in the way he nuzzled her neck, made her heart beat a little faster.

He lifted his head and pressed his forehead to hers, eyelids heavy as he looked down at her. "Okay, I lied."

"About what?"

"I want to kiss you. I've been thinking about it almost constantly for the past two days."

The thrill she felt knowing he wanted her seemed to cancel out any shred of her common sense. "So, kiss me."

She didn't have to tell him twice. And, oh, could he kiss. If she never kissed another man as long as she lived, she would go to her grave knowing she could never find anyone who did it better. And something told her that this time it wouldn't end there.

She didn't want it to.

He let go of her to take his jacket off, then he pushed her coat off her shoulders to the floor. When he started to unfasten the buttons on her jacket, she knew in the back of her mind there was a reason this was wrong, why she should tell him to stop, but for the life of her she couldn't remember why. She didn't *want* to remember.

He pulled her jacket open but he didn't take it off. Instead he gazed down at her, tracing a finger along her skin just above the silk shell she was wearing. "You are so beautiful, Jane."

He made her *feel* beautiful. As if she deserved this.

He dipped his finger below the shell to caress the uppermost swell of her breasts. First the left, then the right, and her breath started coming faster.

"If you're going to tell me to stop, do it now," he said, his voice rough. "Because I'm about two minutes from taking you into your bedroom and making love to you."

She fisted his shirt and tugged it from the waist of his pants. "It's the second door on the right."

With a look that could melt snow, he scooped her off her feet and carried her—actually *carried* her—down the hall to her bedroom. A little voice asked her what the heck she thought she was doing. She wasn't actually going to sleep with him, was she? Because that was against the rules. But for the first time in her entire life she didn't care about the rules. She wanted to do something totally illogical and completely spontaneous. She didn't care if it was bad for her, as long as it felt good.

Jordan set her on her feet beside the bed and she kicked off her shoes. "We need light," he said.

She switched the lamp on, hoping, as she tugged her jacket off, then pulled her top over her head, he wasn't disappointed by what he saw. Did she look as good as he made her feel?

"Don't stop there," he said, unbuttoning his shirt as he watched her. "Keep going."

She had never done a striptease for anyone, but he filled her with a confidence she'd never felt before. And maybe it was wrong, but she would do just about anything right now to make him happy.

She reached back to unzip her skirt, thankful, as she wiggled out of it, that she'd worn her matching black lace bra and panties. His low growl as his gaze slipped down to her legs said he was a man who appreciated thigh-high stockings.

"The bra too," he said, watching her intently. If she didn't know any better, she might think he was challenging her, seeing just how far he could push. Maybe he was.

She undid the clasp and slipped it off, then hooked her thumbs in the waist of her panties and eased them down, but when she reached for the elastic edge of the thigh-high he shook his head. "Those can stay. My turn now."

She waited for him to start undressing, and when he didn't, when he grinned and said, "What are you waiting for?" she realized that he wanted *her* to undress him.

He'd probably been with dozens of women, most more experienced or well-versed in making love than she was, but she didn't care. She was here now. And she knew somewhere deep down that this was special. He had picked *her*.

His shirt was already unbuttoned, so she pushed it off his shoulders. He was so beautiful, so *perfect*.

He fished his wallet from his back pocket and tossed it on the bedside table. Probably because that was where he kept the condoms, and they were going to be needing one. The thought made her knees go weak. She was really going to do it, she was going to sleep with him.

"Keep going," he said.

She unhooked his belt then unfastened his pants, pushing them down. He kicked them, and his shoes out of the way, then bent over to pull his socks off. All that was left was his boxers, and if the tent in the front was any indiction, she was going to like what she found underneath.

"On or off," he said. "Your call."

Why did she get the feeling he thought she wouldn't do it? The old Jane would probably be afraid. She would be worried that she would do something wrong and disappoint him. But this was the new Jane, and she was no longer afraid of anything.

She grasped the elastic waistband and pulled them down, then she circled his erection in her hand and squeezed. He groaned and heat pulsed against her palm. She smiled up at him and said, "Off."

She felt like she would go crazy if he didn't touch her soon, and he didn't make her wait. He sat back on the bed and pulled her down with him, rolling her over so that she was on her back and he was looking down at her. Then he kissed her, and she felt so hot with lust, if not for her skin holding her together, she would have melted into the sheets.

He didn't hedge or fumble. He knew exactly what to do to drive her crazy without her ever having to utter a word. His solitary goal, as far as she could tell, was to give her as much pleasure as possible, as many times as possible, before he would even think about himself.

She'd heard that men like him existed, but she honestly believed it was a myth, that those women who bragged about their generous lovers were all lying through their teeth and really had the same boring and pathetically unsatisfying sex lives as she did.

Boy, had she been wrong.

It seemed like forever before he finally grabbed his wallet and pulled out a condom. He pushed her thighs apart and knelt between them, dangling the package in front of her. "Care to do the honors?"

She'd never actually "done the honors" before but if that was what he wanted she would try. She didn't even care if she fumbled a bit. And somehow she didn't think he would either.

She took the packet from him and tore it open with her teeth. As she rolled it down the length of him he closed his eyes and sucked in a breath, digging his fingers into the meat of her calves. She probably took a little longer than necessary, but he wasn't complaining.

When she was finished she asked, "Is that right?"

He opened his eyes and gazed down at her handiwork. "Looks good to me." He grinned and added, "Felt good too."

He lowered himself over her. "Are you ready?"

She was ready the minute he walked through the door.

She wrapped her legs around his waist, pulling him closer, and with his eyes locked on hers, he slowly thrust inside of her. She had some random, fleeting thought about how this wasn't supposed to be happening, but as he groaned and thrust again, the last remnants of doubt fizzled away. And as he rolled over on to his back, pulling her on top of him, all that she cared about was making him feel good.

It was no-holds-barred, pulse-pounding, headboard-banging, twisted-in-the-sheets, rolling-all-over-the-bed sex. And it was *fun*. She had no idea that sex was supposed to be fun.

Afterward, they both lay flat on their backs, side by side, limp and satisfied. And only then did the possible repercussions of her lack of good sense hit her square between the eyes.

What had his brother Nathan told her? Jordan had a short attention span when it came to women. He liked the chase, but once he got what he was after, he lost interest. So of course, genius that she was, she'd gone and given him exactly what he wanted with practically no effort on his part whatsoever.

Brilliant.

In one act of pure idiocy she had compromised her

principles, crossed the lines of morality and put the investigation in the toilet.

Way to go, Jane.

There had to be a way to begin repairing the damage she'd done. A good start would be to get him the heck out of her bed, back into his clothes and out the door. That was when she realized how quiet he'd become. She pushed herself up on her elbows to look at him. His eyes were closed.

"Jordan?"

He didn't answer. She gave his arm a gentle nudge, and when that got no response, she gave it a shake. Nothing. He was out cold. He had actually rolled over and gone to sleep.

How was that for a cliché?

Of course, considering he'd barely slept for two days, and then had a vigorous workout, she could hardly fault him; besides, that was the least of her worries. The sad fact was, she wouldn't be sleeping with him again.

She shook him again. "Jordan, wake up."

He mumbled something incoherent and rolled onto his side.

It looked as though she had no choice but to let him stay the night, since nothing short of a dousing with ice water was going to wake him. And though she doubted he would rouse anytime soon, just in case, she would have to leave her makeup on, so he didn't see how she actually looked. Then he would *really* lose interest.

He didn't budge when she untangled his feet from the blankets and covered them both, nor when she leaned over him to switch off the light. She lay there wide awake beside him, listening to his slow, deep breaths, plotting her next move.

She sighed. It was going to be a really long night.

Ten

The smell of coffee woke Jordan from a dead sleep. He opened his eyes, confused for a second by the unfamiliar room, then he remembered last night and smiled. He rolled over and reached for Jane, but her side of the bed was empty and cold.

Rubbing the sleep from his eyes, and some moisture into his contacts, he grabbed his watch from the bedside table and squinted to read it. Seven-thirty. He should have been up over an hour ago. But he was having a tough time caring, considering how freaking incredible last night had been.

He'd come here with the expectation of some harmless necking, and thought—or hoped—that if he played his cards right he might cop a feel or two. Well, so much for her so-called lack of confidence with men. He'd been with supermodels who were nowhere close to as comfortable in their own skin as Jane had seemed to be last night. She had completely blown him away, surpassing by leaps and bounds every preconceived notion he had drawn since she stumbled into his life Monday morning.

The idea of the timid and apprehensive Jane had intrigued him, but the real Jane fascinated and bewitched him.

He shoved himself up out of bed, grabbed his clothes from the floor and got dressed, then followed the scent of coffee to the kitchen.

Jane was sitting at the table, already primped and dressed for work, drinking coffee and working on her laptop.

"Good morning."

She looked up and smiled. "Good morning. There's coffee. Can I get you a cup?"

"I'll get it," he said, pressing a kiss to the top of her head as he walked past. There was already a cup and the creamer waiting on the counter beside the coffee press. "Sorry I conked out like that last night. I don't even remember falling asleep."

"I figured you were pretty tired."

"So tired I didn't even take my contacts out," he said as he fixed his coffee.

"You wear contacts?"

"Since college when I finally ditched the glasses. Without them I'm blind as a bat." He carried his coffee to the table and sat across from her. Maybe it was his imagination, but there was a weird vibe. Not the typical "morning after" glow. At least not what he would expect after an evening of sex that was, if he was being totally honest, about as good as it ever got.

Jane closed her laptop and pushed it aside. "I wear the kind you can leave in, so I don't have to take them out."

"Me too, but it feels good to take them out every few

days. Especially when I haven't gotten much sleep." He sipped his coffee, then set the cup down and asked, "So, is there a reason we're discussing contact lenses and not what happened last night?"

She cradled her cup in her palms, running her thumbs along the brim. "Last night was...*wow*."

"Yes it was."

"It meant more to me than you could possibly imagine."

Oh boy. If she was about to tell him that she loved him he would have a serious problem.

He must have looked uneasy, because she smiled and said, "Don't worry, I'm not picking out china patterns or anything. It's completely the opposite. I feel as if I've been walking around with my eyes closed, and being with you has finally opened them."

"I'm not sure I follow you."

"This is a little embarrassing, but, Drake was my first serious boyfriend."

"Serious, as in..."

"He's the only man I ever slept with. And it was never... Well, let's just say it was *nothing* like last night. I had no idea it could be so...so..."

"Remarkable?"

"*Yes!* All this time I had no idea what I was missing. And if I had married Drake, I never would have known." She reached across the table and put her hand over his. "For a long time I've just been drifting. I didn't know that there was more to life, so I didn't even bother trying to find something better. Now I feel as if I'm actually ready to move on. Meet new people and take chances. I feel like there's someone out there who can actually make me happy."

Someone other than him, she meant.

That was harsh. Especially for her, who didn't seem

to have a vindictive or mean bone in her body. Every time he thought he had her pegged, she did something to completely blow his perception. Or was this an act? A part of her cover. Or did she really feel that way? Either way, it worked just fine for him, because he didn't do forever. He didn't even do long-term.

"So what you're saying is you're dumping me. After one night?"

"Come on, Jordan, you can't dump someone that you aren't technically with. I like you. I could probably love you. But there's just no future for us. It's not what you want. You're not a forever kind of guy, and that's what I'm looking for. What I need."

This was the part when he should be relieved that she was giving him an out, so he wouldn't have to break her heart later. So why instead did he feel…slighted?

"I'm almost thirty. If I'm going to have a family I have to start thinking about settling down. Oh, and speaking of settling down…" she let go of his hand "…look what came in yesterday's mail."

He took the white card she held out. It was an invitation. For Drake and Megan's wedding. "Wow. How totally inappropriate."

"I know. What moron thinks it's okay to invite the woman he dumped for his fiancée to the wedding? It defies logic."

"Not if you're an arrogant ass."

"I keep thinking about how it must have made Megan feel that he even wanted to invite me. I actually feel sorry for her. Granted, she's not the sharpest tool in the shed, but she's a sweet person."

"Should I assume you won't be attending?"

"Are you kidding? I won't even justify it with a response. But you're right, I do need to go to the reunion. To show him that I really don't care about him anymore, because honestly, I don't."

"I'd still be happy to go as your date."

"I think this is something I need to do on my own. And under the circumstances, I don't think it would be a good idea. But that doesn't mean I wouldn't like us to be friends."

How many women had he used a variation of that exact line on? Probably too many to count. To date, he was friends with none of them.

What if he didn't want to be "friends"? What if he wanted more?

As far as he could tell, he had two choices. He could honor her wishes and back off, or he could agree with her, tell her they could be friends, then seduce her anyway.

Jane sat at her desk, finishing up a few last minute things so she could meet her family for dinner. She glanced over at Jordan's office. Other than a short lunch meeting, he'd been in there all day with the door shut.

She had been stressing all day, worried that she'd overdone it with her let's-just-be-friends speech that morning. She hoped that by turning him down, she would actually make him want her more. That he would see it as a challenge. Telling him that she was looking for a serious relationship had been a risky move, but she had given it a lot of thought and she was confident it would do the trick.

At least, she was *trying* to be confident. Deep down she was terrified that she had completely blown it. All she could do now was wait for his next move. The ball was in his court.

At six-thirty she shut down her computer, grabbed her coat and purse, then rapped on Jordan's door.

"Come in," he called, so she opened it. He was at his desk, engrossed in whatever was on his computer screen.

"I just wanted to let you know that I'm leaving for the night," she said.

"Okay," he said, glancing up at her. "I'll see you Monday."

"See you Monday." She closed the door, frowning. She had half expected him to mention the date that they were supposed to go on Saturday night, and maybe suggest that they go as friends.

He was taking her brush-off a little too well.

She walked to her car, a knot in the pit of her belly. In her attempt to fix this, had she only made matters worse?

It wasn't until she was at the restaurant, and caught a glimpse of her reflection in the glass door, that she remembered her family hadn't yet seen her new look. The suit and high heels she couldn't do much about, but she could probably slip into the ladies room and remove her makeup before going to the table.

Take off her makeup? What was she, a *child?*

No, she was an adult woman who had just as much right to wear makeup as anyone else, and wear whatever clothes she wanted. Whatever weird hold her family still had over her, it needed to stop.

Besides, knowing them, they probably wouldn't even notice.

The hostess took her coat and she walked to the table, where everyone was already seated and had been served drinks. And contrary to what she had anticipated, there were no birthday balloons or banners. No gifts in sight.

Well, that didn't mean they weren't going to celebrate. "Hi everyone. Sorry I'm late."

Everyone looked up to greet her, and seven jaws dropped in perfect unison.

Okay, so maybe they would notice.

Mary was the first to find her voice. "Oh my God, are you wearing *makeup?*" she asked, as if Jane had just committed some unforgivable crime. Both Mary and her mother were wearing makeup and no one seemed to have a problem with that.

"Yeah, so what?" she said, sliding into the empty chair beside her sister and setting her purse on the floor by her feet.

"What did you do to your hair?" her oldest brother Richard asked.

"I had it styled." She opened her menu. "Have we decided what we're ordering?"

"What's with the suit?" her brother Will asked. "Did you come from a costume party or something? And where are your glasses?"

A costume party. Nice.

She glared at him. "I traded my glasses in for contacts, and the suit is new."

"Is this about Drake?" her father asked. "I heard that he's engaged."

He would have to bring that up. "This has nothing to do with Drake or anyone else. I just felt like I needed a change. And I don't appreciate getting the third degree."

"Can you blame us for being curious, sweetheart?" her mom said. "We hardly see you, then you come in looking so…different. Sometimes I feel as if I don't even know you anymore."

Was it too much to expect her family to be happy for her, or at least support her decisions? Why did everything have to be a fight with them? It seemed as though whatever she did lately they saw as a further departure from the fold.

"I think she looks fabulous," Richard's wife, Cyan, announced, and Jane sent her a grateful smile. "That suit is super-chic and I love the new hairstyle. The cut and color really complement your complexion and the shape of your face. And the shade of shadow you're wearing really makes your eyes pop."

Cyan was the owner of a fashion consulting firm that catered to the uber-wealthy and chic, so the compliment really meant something coming from her.

"I think she does too," Sara piped in. A quiet and unassuming first grade teacher, Will's wife tended to fade into the background during family functions. Sort of like an adorable potted plant. It wasn't easy competing for attention with a bunch of outspoken, power-hungry professionals. Jane knew. She had been trying most of her life, but she lacked the killer instinct. Which is probably why she'd let her family roll over her and make her decisions for her for so many years, and why they felt so threatened now that she was finally gaining her independence.

"I don't think anyone is suggesting that Jane doesn't look good," her dad said, shooting Sara a look that made her shrink low in her chair. Always pick on the weakest, that was her family's motto. "We're just concerned."

"Are you having some sort of premidlife crisis?" Richard asked.

"Can we just drop this?" Jane asked.

"You don't have to be such a bitch about it," Mary mumbled and Jane had the very immature inclination to pull her hair. It was her freaking birthday for God's sake, or at least it had been Tuesday, and not a single one of them had even acknowledged it.

The waiter appeared to take their food orders and along with the lasagna she doubted she would even eat, she ordered a pomegranate martini. After he left, the conversation turned to the family practice, which under normal circumstances would irritate her, but she was just relieved they were no longer focused on her. She ordered a second martini when the salad was served, then another when the main course arrived. At the rate she was going, she'd have to take a cab home.

She picked at her dinner, trying not to let it depress her that despite what she'd believed, they really didn't plan to celebrate her birthday. Her entire family had forgotten. The minute they had gotten over the initial shock of her new appearance, she was back to being invisible. They didn't even ask her about work, or what she'd been up to.

Jane decided that she would duck out before everyone ordered an after-dinner drink. She opened her mouth to tell them she was going, when behind her someone said, "Jane?"

At the sound of the familiar voice, her heart plummeted. In an instant this dinner went from sad and depressing to her worst nightmare.

She turned in her seat, hoping it just sounded like him, but was actually someone else, and for a second she thought maybe it was. In faded jeans, cowboy boots and a black, untucked shirt with the sleeves rolled up, Jordan looked like a regular guy—albeit a breathtakingly gorgeous one.

"I thought that was you," he said.

She shot up from her chair. "Jordan…hi."

This could not be happening. Her undercover assignment did not just walk in on dinner with her *entire* family! "What are you doing here?"

"I was in the bar, having drinks with a friend. I was just getting ready to leave when I thought I saw you sitting there." He flashed her a grin that made her stomach flop. "Small world, huh?"

One hell of a lot smaller than she'd ever imagined.

Although she had the sneaking suspicion that their bumping into one another was no accident.

Yes, she had hoped he would pursue her, but not in the middle of a family dinner!

"Honey," her father said. "Aren't you going to introduce us to your friend?"

Jane realized everyone at the table was watching them. Figures that *now* they would notice her. Although it was Jordan they were focused on.

She had no choice but to introduce him.

"This is Jordan Everette. Jordan, this is my family."

He shook hands with everyone, and she hoped that once the introductions were out of the way, he would leave.

"Jordan, why don't you pull up a chair, have a drink," her father said.

"I don't want to intrude."

"Don't be silly," her mother said, in her sweet, Southern-belle tone. "We would love it if you'd join us."

"In that case I'd be happy to."

Crap.

He pulled up a chair from a neighboring table and sat beside Jane, lounging casually, so close their thighs were practically touching. She wished he would back off a little. She didn't want her parents to get the impression that they were involved.

Her father signaled the waiter and everyone ordered drinks. Jordan asked for a Chivas on the rocks. Jane ordered another martini.

"So, do you and Jane work together?" Rick asked Jordan.

Jane's pulse started to hammer. She had told Jordan about how she was deceiving her family about her job, but if he slipped up and said something about them working together at Western Oil, she was dead meat.

"No, I'm in the oil business," Jordan told him.

She was so relieved that if she hadn't been sitting, her legs would have given out.

"What do you do?" Will asked.

"I'm in management."

Jane could see everyone digesting that information. Her family could smell money and power a mile away, and though Jordan wasn't dressed like an executive, and he was young, the platinum Rolex on his left wrist said he was either old money, or at least upper middle management. They probably figured he pulled in a salary in the low to middle six figures. And she wasn't about to set them straight.

"So, are you two dating?" Mary asked.

"Mary!" Jane snapped.

"I've asked her out," Jordan said, grinning adorably, draping his arm over the back of her chair and pinning her with that judgment-wrecking gaze. "But she turned me down."

He was obviously teasing her. She just wished he would do it from a little farther away. The scent of his aftershave was shorting out her brain. His looks he couldn't really help, but he could at least have the decency not to smell so darned good.

She tore her gaze from Jordan's and turned to her sister. "We're just friends."

The waiter brought their drinks, then Jordan asked about the law practice, and that became the focus of the conversation. Though her defection from the fold was mentioned, thankfully no one dwelled on it. In fact, her name didn't come up much at all. But of course her parents didn't hesitate to sing the praises of her sister and brothers and their many legal accomplishments. But what else was new? Jane may have had more of her own accomplishments if they hadn't continually held her back. She was hands down a better attorney than her sister, yet Mary had been allowed to build an impressive client base while Jane had been given the grunt work.

She was sure they were all curious as to why someone so charming and personable and devastatingly attractive would have any interest in being friends with someone like her. Maybe that was why Mary flirted shamelessly the entire time. Maybe she thought that because he and Jane were just friends, it was okay. Or maybe she was doing it to show her up. It wouldn't be the first time.

Jane had skipped two grades, so she was only one grade behind her sister in high school, and it never failed, if she showed any interest in a boy, Mary would go after him with all pistons firing. And if Jane complained, Mary's answer was always the same. "What's the big deal? It's not as if he would ever go out with *you*."

And she was right. But that didn't make it hurt any less, or make Jane feel any less betrayed.

After a second round of drinks, Jordan said he had to go.

"It's early," her mother said. "There's no need to rush off."

"Yes, you should stay," her father said.

"I really need to go." He pushed up from his chair. "It was a pleasure meeting everyone."

"The pleasure was ours," her father said, shaking his hand.

"I hope we'll see you again," her mother said, shooting Jane a look that said she was out of her mind for not snapping him up and marrying him at the first possible opportunity.

"It was really nice meeting you," Mary said, shaking his hand and holding it several seconds longer than Jane considered appropriate. Would it be totally immature to give her a good hard knock in the head?

When she finally let go, Jordan turned to Jane. "I guess I'll see you around."

Jane knew that if she stayed after he left, she would be subjected to the third degree all over again. She didn't like being ignored, but being grilled wasn't a whole lot of fun either. There was no happy medium with her family. Leaving with Jordan was her only chance for escape, so she hopped to her feet and said, "I should get going too. I'll walk out with you."

Eleven

"Are you sure?" Jordan asked.

She was *so* sure. "Yeah, I should get home. It's been a busy week and I'm exhausted."

She said a quick goodbye to her family, who didn't even implore her to stay. Nice. It was great to know that they cared.

Only as she walked away from the table did she realize just how tipsy she was feeling. When she and Jordan got to the lobby, and were waiting for the hostess to fetch their coats, she leaned up against the wall for stability.

"Your family seems nice," Jordan said.

"Yeah. They do *seem* nice."

His brow rose. "Are you suggesting that they aren't?"

"They're a family of extremes. Either they're demanding and bossy and trying to run my life, or they ignore me completely."

"You know that your sister is jealous of you."

She laughed. "Jealous of what? She's pretty and successful."

"And she obviously doesn't like you having something that she can't."

"What do you mean?"

He reached into his jeans pocket and handed her a business card. *Mary's* business card. "She stuck it in my hand when I was saying goodbye."

Jane shook her head. Un-freaking-believable. Clearly nothing had changed.

She tried to hand the card back to him and he said, "You keep it. I won't be needing it."

That made her smile.

The hostess appeared with their coats and when Jordan helped her into hers, she nearly lost her balance.

"You okay?" he asked, grabbing her arm to steady her.

"Yeah, I think I had two or three martinis too many. My family often has that effect on me."

"Then you shouldn't be driving."

"I would never drive impaired. I'll call a cab."

"Why would you pay for a cab when I can give you a lift home? I'll even arrange to have your car delivered to you so you don't have to come back and get it."

It would be silly to turn down the ride. Now that she knew she still had his interest, she had to be sure to keep it. Without overplaying her hand this time. "That would be great, thanks."

He ushered her outside and handed his valet slip to the attendant, who dashed off and pulled up a minute later in a shiny silver sports car that looked a little like the Batmobile. And very expensive. It was exactly the sort of car she pictured Jordan driving.

He helped her in, then walked around and got in the driver's side. The interior was dark gray leather and smelled like a mix of new car and Jordan's cologne. A country station was playing on the radio, which surprised her a little. He struck her as more of the classic rock type.

"So, what kind of car is this?" she asked as he pulled out of the lot and zipped into traffic.

"A Porsche Spyder Coupe."

"It's nice."

"Thanks."

"How much does a car like this cost, if you don't mind my asking."

"Six hundred and some change," he said, downshifting to turn a corner.

"Six hundred *thousand?* That's... Wow."

He looked over at her and grinned. "Yeah, but it makes me look good."

It sure did. And it was a testament to just how loaded he was. He was so easygoing and unpretentious, she sometimes forgot the magnitude of his wealth and power. And for whatever reason, he wanted *her.*

The thought made her smile.

"So, I figured you would be celebrating your birthday with your family tonight."

The smile slipped from her face. "Yeah, me too."

He glanced over at her. "Are you saying that they *forgot?*"

She shrugged and said, "It's not a big deal." And if she kept telling herself that, maybe she would start believing it.

"Have you ever forgotten one of their birthdays?"

Of course not. She was reliable Jane. "I think it's my punishment for leaving the practice, for going against their wishes. Sometimes they act like I'm not even a part of the family any longer."

He reached over and brushed her hair back from her

face. It was such a sweet gesture, for some stupid reason it made her feel like crying. But she was not the crying type, so it must have been the alcohol.

"Families suck," he said.

Wasn't that the truth. She was so tired of feeling as if she wasn't good enough, as though what she wanted, and her happiness, didn't matter. She sighed and laid her head back, letting her eyes drift closed. She listened to the melody playing softly on the radio, and Jordan's voice singing slightly off-key with Keith Urban.

She must have drifted off, because the next thing she knew, Jordan was calling her name and nudging her awake.

Jane's eyes fluttered open and she bolted upright. "I'm sorry. Did I fall asleep?"

"It's okay," Jordan said, rubbing her shoulder. "We're here."

She looked out the windshield, a frown creasing her brow. "Um…where is *here?*"

He cut the engine. "The parking garage of my building."

"I thought you were taking me home."

"I did. To my home."

She shot him an exasperated look.

He grinned. "I'm sorry, did you want me to take you to *your* home?"

She shook her head and laughed, as if she thought he was hopeless. "Yeah, that was the idea."

He liked making her smile, making her happy. "Well, in my defense, you never actually specified. But since you're already here, you may as well come up and have a look around." After all, that was probably part of her plan to get information. She must have figured out by now that there was nothing in his office to suggest he had anything to do with the sabotage. Logically the next place to look would be his home. Not that she would find anything there either, but she could try. He wanted her to know that he would never do anything to hurt anyone. He didn't even know why he cared. He just did.

"Jordan—"

"Listen, it's nine o'clock on a Friday night and you're clearly upset. What kind of friend would I be if I let you spend the evening alone watching Arnold Schwarzenegger, scarfing caramel nut swirl ice cream."

He could tell by her expression, that was exactly what she would have done.

"You must think I'm an idiot for even caring what they think," she said.

He draped his arm over the back of her seat, leaning in. "Jane, I just spent two days at the bedside of a mother who missed my high school graduation because she had a hair appointment."

"Seriously?"

"Seriously. So who do you think is the bigger idiot?"

For a long moment she just looked at him, searching his face. "How do you do it?"

"Do what?"

"Always manage to say exactly the right thing," she said, then she slipped her hand behind his neck, pulled him closer and kissed him. It was the last thing he expected. He thought he was going to have to work for it, seduce her into seeing things his way. He wasn't sure *what* he'd done but obviously it had worked.

She broke the kiss and gazed up at him. "Take me upstairs, Jordan, right now, before I change my mind."

"Let's go."

They got out of the car and crossed the garage to the elevator. The second they were inside, and the doors slid closed, her arms were around him and her lips were on his.

He had kissed a lot of women, but no one put more heart and soul into it. More honesty. If he were a better man, he would take into consideration the fact that she was slightly compromised by the drinks, and maybe not thinking one hundred percent clearly, but as she rubbed her hand over the crotch of his jeans she seemed to know exactly what she wanted. And there was no question for him either.

The doors opened at the top floor. He grabbed her hand and pulled her into the foyer of his penthouse.

"You own the entire top floor?" she asked.

"I own the building. I live on the top floor." He punched his code into the pad and opened the door, pulling her inside. It was dark, but for the lamp next to the couch.

"Wow," Jane said, taking in the open-concept space, tugging her jacket off and draping it across the back of an overstuffed chair. "This is nice. It's not at all what I expected."

He did the same with his jacket. "What did you expect?"

"Something more modern. Glass and steel and black leather. And I like the dark wood and the earth tones, and the furniture looks so soft and comfortable" She unbuttoned the jacket of her suit and tossed that on the chair too. She wore another one of those sleeveless, silky numbers underneath. "It's so…homey and warm."

"Thanks," he said, unbuttoning his shirt. "I've always believed a house should be a home. Although I can't really take credit. I hired a decorator."

She nodded to the bank of windows across the room, clearly dazzled by the panoramic view of the city. "The view is amazing."

"It's the main reason I bought the building."

She pulled her top over her head and dropped it on the growing pile. She wore a sheer white bra underneath. Her breasts were on the small side, but what she had was so beautiful, he didn't care. He had always been more of a leg man, and hers were long and lean and perfect, especially when they were wrapped around his waist. Or his shoulders, or pretty much any part of his body.

She unzipped her skirt and pushed it down her legs. Under it she wore a matching thong and, hot damn, those thigh-high stockings.

She grabbed the front of his shirt, backed herself against the wall beside the door and pulled him in for a kiss. And damn could she kiss. She pushed the shirt off his shoulders and he tugged it down his arms. She arched her back, rubbing her lace-covered breasts against his chest, devouring his mouth. He slipped a hand inside her panties and she moaned, biting down on his lower lip. He dipped into her wet heat, teasing her with feather-light strokes.

Her breath was coming harder and faster. He yanked the cup of her bra down and licked the tip of her breast, then he sucked it into his mouth. She gasped and her head fell back. Since she seemed to like it, he did the same thing to the other side. She moaned and started to shake all over, then her body clamped down hard around his fingers. He'd been with women it took forever to satisfy, until it was more of a chore than actual fun. Jane was not one of those women.

"Maybe we should move this to my bedroom," he said.

She gazed up at him with lust glazed eyes and tugged his pants open. "No, right here. Against the wall."

"Condoms are in the bedroom."

She shoved his pants down and he kicked them off. "I've got it covered."

"You're on the pill?"

"IUD."

Good enough for him. He slid her panties down and she stepped out of them, then he lifted her off her feet, pinning her hard against the wall. She gasped and clamped her legs around his waist, wrapped her arms around his neck. He was afraid he might have hurt her, but her smile said she liked it. Despite her willowy physique, she was no delicate flower. She liked it a little rough; she wasn't afraid to experiment either.

His eyes locked on hers. He thrust inside of her, and without the condom to dull the sensation, the pleasure was so intense he nearly lost it. He tried to keep a slow, steady pace, but that just didn't seem to be cutting it. Jane clawed her fingers through his hair, bumping her hips in time with his thrusts, moaning, *"Harder."* He had no choice but to give her what she wanted, and when her muscles clamped around him and she moaned with release again, he tried to hold back, but seeing her look of utter bliss did him in.

"Just when I think it can't get any better, it does," she said breathlessly, still clinging to him.

He dropped his head on her shoulder, breathing hard. "Have I mentioned how good you are for my ego?"

She laughed. "I seriously doubt your ego needs any help from me. I think you're probably the most confident man I've ever met in my life."

"And I'm more irresistible than I thought. I brought you here with every intention of seducing you, but you beat me to it."

"I guess after five years of mediocre sex, then nine months of no sex at all, maybe I feel as if I deserve a little fun."

His knees were close to buckling, so he carried Jane the five feet to the couch and sat down with her in his lap. "Is that all this is? Fun?"

She loosened her arms from around his neck, gazing at him with a puzzled look. "Where else do you see this going?"

He shrugged. "I don't know. All I do know is that one night with you wasn't enough. Call me selfish, but I wanted more."

"How much more?"

"I don't know."

"A day, a week?"

A lifetime? The way he was feeling tonight, he couldn't imagine ever *not* wanting her. He barely knew her, yet he felt more connected to her than he'd ever felt to a woman. He didn't even care that every so often she had to lie to him. That had to mean something, right?

"I don't know how long." He reached up, stroked her cheek. "All I know is that everything in me is telling me that *right now,* this is what I need."

"The same rules apply. No one can know. Not our families or our friends. And especially not the people at work."

"Why?"

She sighed. "Because that's what *I* need."

Did he honestly think she was going to tell him the truth? That sleeping with a man she was investigating would get her fired. And who was he to judge her? By not telling her he knew who she really was, wasn't he being just as dishonest? But the truth was going to come out eventually. He could only hope that when it did, they would have grown tired of each other. They could move on with their lives and no one would be hurt.

"That means no more following me to dinners with my family."

He opened his mouth to deny it, and she held up a hand to shush him. "Don't insult my intelligence. That was a little too coincidental. And trust me when I say that getting to know my family is a headache that you don't want. If they think we're dating, and they find out who you are, once they get past the shock of someone like you dating someone like me, they're going to be planning our wedding."

"What do you mean, someone like me dating someone like you? Do you really think I'm that shallow?"

"Isn't that what you like people to think?"

She had him there. It was just easier that way. And hell, maybe he was a little shallow.

"I'll stay away from your family," he said.

"Thank you."

His stomach rumbled loudly, and Jane grinned. "Hungry?"

"I skipped dinner."

"The truth is, I didn't do much more than pick at mine. Being with my family has a way of killing my appetite."

"We could order in."

"And eat naked in bed? I've always wanted to do that."

Her honest enthusiasm made him smile. "Anywhere you want."

And when they were finished eating, he was going to spend the rest of the evening making love to her.

Twelve

Despite being up half the night making love, Jane woke at her usual six-thirty the next morning—with a very naked, very warm, and very aroused male form curled up behind her.

Tempted as she was to roll over and wake Jordan in a very pleasurable way—of which she could imagine several—this would be the perfect opportunity to do some snooping. Other than the living area and his bedroom, she hadn't seen much of the apartment. The one room she was most interested in finding was his office.

Her heart thumping with adrenaline, she slipped out of bed. Jordan mumbled in his sleep and rolled onto his back. Her clothes were still in a pile by the front door, so she tiptoed across the cool wood floor to his closet to look for something to wear. It was pitch-black, so she stepped inside and switched on the light, and when she saw her reflection in the floor-to-ceiling mirror across the room she actually gasped.

Her hair was a tangled mess, the mineral foundation had completely worn off, leaving her horrible freckles exposed, and what little was left of her eyeliner and mascara was smeared below her eyes. Thank God she'd woken before Jordan. If he had seen her like this, for who she really was—boring Plain Jane—he wouldn't be so eager to continue their affair.

She grabbed a button-down shirt off a hanger and slipped it on, then she switched off the light and peeked out into the bedroom. Jordan was still sound asleep. She crept back to the bed where she'd left her purse and snatched it up off the floor. Thank goodness she kept her makeup with her at all times. She made her way quietly to the bathroom and stepped inside, leaving the door open just a crack, so the snap of it closing didn't wake him.

She switched on the light and dug through her purse for her hairbrush, using it to tug the tangles from her hair, which of course left it limp and lifeless. She flipped her head over and gave it a firm brushing in the hopes that she could beat at least a little bit of body into it. Then she fluffed it into place. Not great, but not awful either. But she really had to do something with her face.

She found a rag and a hand towel in the closet and began to scrub off the remnants of last night's makeup. *One should always begin with a clean canvas,* the makeup artist had told her. She dried off and scowled at her reflection. A couple of weeks ago she wouldn't have thought twice about going to work this way, but now she could barely stand the sight of her naked face.

She pulled her makeup bag out and fished through it for her mineral foundation and applicator brush. She opened the jar and dipped the brush in, tapping the excess off, then raised it to her cheek—

"Good morning."

She jerked in surprise at the sound of Jordan's voice and the brush slipped from her fingers. It dropped to the granite countertop, leaving a poof of mineral powder, then bounced over the side, hit the toilet seat and rolled into the bowl with a soft sploosh.

Crap. What was she supposed to do now?

"What are you doing?" Jordan asked, leaning in the doorway looking rumpled and sexy, wearing nothing but silk boxers and a smile.

She cupped her hands over her naked face, since there wasn't much else she could do. "Could I have a minute, please?"

He looked at the brush in the toilet, then the makeup bag. "Are you putting on makeup?"

"Yes," she mumbled through her fingers.

"It's six-forty on a Saturday morning."

"I know what time it is."

"So come back to bed."

"Just let me fix my face."

"Why?"

"Take my word, you don't want to see me this way."

His expression went from amused to puzzled. "You're serious."

"Very. So please, get lost and let me finish."

He folded his arms over that ridiculously toned chest. "No."

"I'm not kidding, Jordan, leave."

"You've piqued my interest. Now I *have* to see."

He was blocking the doorway so running wasn't an option, and he outweighed her by at least sixty pounds, the majority of it muscle, so forcing her way past him wasn't going to work either.

"Jordan, *please,*" she said, feeling desperate.

"I'm not leaving," he said, "so you may as well drop your hands."

This was it, she thought. The end of her career at the agency. He was going to see how she really looked and realize the woman he'd been having an affair with was a fraud.

Feeling resigned and defeated, she dropped her hands to her sides. Jordan's eyes searched her face and she steeled herself for the look of disappointment. The indignation of a man who was known for dating supermodels and beauty queens realizing that he'd been tricked into bed with Plain Jane Monroe.

Instead, a grin curled his mouth and he said, "You have freckles."

Her hands flew back up to cover her face, and mortified, she turned away from him. "I hate them."

"That wasn't an insult," he said with a laugh. "I think they're adorable."

"They're awful. *I* look awful."

"What are you talking about? You're beautiful, Jane."

"You don't have to lie to me to save my feelings. I know what I look like."

He stepped behind her and wrapped his hands around her wrists, forcing her to face the mirror, then he tugged her hands away from her face and held them at her sides. She averted her eyes, but he said, "Look at yourself."

Reluctantly she gazed at her reflection.

"Tell me what you see."

"Nobody. Without the makeup I'm so plain, so boring, I might as well not exist."

"Is that what you really think, or is that your family talking?"

Not just her family. Everyone.

"It isn't makeup that makes a person beautiful, Jane. It's what's on the inside." He let go of her wrists and turned her to face him. "And you are the sweetest, most passionate, and most *beautiful* woman I have ever met." He laid his hand on her chest. "Because of what's in here."

Did he really see her that way? Did he really appreciate her for who she was on the inside?

"In school they called me Plain Jane."

"Shame on you for believing them."

She smiled and laid her head against his chest and he wrapped his arms around her. She may not have been completely honest with him, but one thing that she told him she meant with all her heart. She could love him. In fact, maybe she already did a little. And it had nothing to do with his wealth and power. In fact, she wanted him in spite of those things. He made her feel good about herself. No one had ever done that before.

"I know how tough it can be, ignoring the hurtful things people say," he said.

"What could anyone say to you that you couldn't refute by looking in a mirror?"

"I want to show you something," he said. He took her hand and led her out of the bedroom and into the next room. He switched on the light and her heart picked up speed when she realized they were in his office. It was the size of the entire living space of her apartment and decorated in rich colors and dark polished wood. Very masculine and surprisingly homey. And considering the clutter, he clearly spent a lot of time there.

If she was going to find anything incriminating, this is where it would be. Or where she would find proof to exonerate him. Because really, that was what she wanted now. She didn't believe for an instant that he was capable of putting anyone's life in danger, much less a whole group of people. He just wasn't that kind of man.

She glanced around the room, taking a mental photo for future reference. Getting the job done might require getting in and out quickly.

She knew that when he found out who she really was he would be furious, and he would probably never forgive her for betraying him, or be able to trust her, but she would at least be able to live with herself knowing that she had helped clear his name.

He pulled a framed eight-by-ten photo off the bookshelf and handed it to her. "It's the ninth grade science fair winners. Guess which one is me."

There were five winners, none of whose faces she could see very clearly. One was a girl, whom she could eliminate because if Jordan had once been a female, Jane would have heard about it by now. That left four boys, who all wore glasses. But one had black hair, so he was out too. The final three had lighter hair and ranged from tall for their age to downright puny. The one in the middle looked pretty average, but with the potential to be cute as an adult, and he'd won first place. She pointed to him. "This one."

"Wrong," Jordan said. "I'm the geek midget who came in third."

Wow. She knew he'd been small for his age, but she never imagined he was *that* small. And yes, he looked pretty geeky, but who didn't at that age? "This is ninth grade," she said. "Everyone goes through an awkward stage."

"Except I looked like that until I was eighteen. Not to mention that I was painfully shy and withdrawn. Which my father thought he could cure by *toughening* me up."

"Toughening you up how?"

"Calling me a sissy, pushing me around. Basically bullying me. And who knows, maybe it would have worked if Nathan hadn't always stepped in to defend me. Even if I had wanted to stand up for myself, he never let me. He would get between me and my dad, get in his face, and it inevitably got physical. Which made me feel guilty."

"Physical?"

"Shoving, punching, backhanding. I can't even tell you how many times Nathan and I got cracked across the mouth when we were kids. My old man was a real bastard back then."

"Where was your mother when this was happening?"

He shrugged. "Somewhere else. She was never much of a mother. It took me years to figure out that her ignoring me was nothing that I'd done. She's just selfish and cold. Well, up until Tuesday anyway. The stroke changed her. But for all I know, once she recovers, she may go back to being her old self."

"It makes my family seem not so bad," she said. "And I have a really hard time trying to imagine you as shy."

"I changed in college. My first year I grew nine inches, and since tall and scrawny was even worse than short and scrawny, I started working out. Girls actually started to notice me, and ask *me* out. It boosted my confidence and drew me out of my shell. I swore I would never be that awkward, insecure kid again."

She handed the photo back to him. "I guess the difference is, I never came out of my shell. At least, not until recently. I never figured out how to be confident. No one ever took me seriously. They still don't."

He set the photo back on the shelf. "But you left the family practice, that took guts."

She wished she could tell him about working at Edwin

Associates, how she had followed her dream. She didn't like that he thought she was nothing more than an office temp, that she was wasting her potential.

"I don't plan to be an office temp forever," she told him. "I'm going to do something big."

"I don't doubt it." He slipped his arms around her, under the shirt, drawing her against him so they were skin to skin. He was so big and warm and strong. She laid her head against his chest, hugging herself close.

"Did I mention how sexy you look wearing my shirt?" he asked. He eased it back off her shoulders, pressing kisses to her neck, and she started to get that electric, tingly-all-over feeling. He slid his hand down to cup her behind, drawing her against him and she could feel that he was getting aroused too.

"I have an idea," he said. "I have to go into work for a while to catch up on a few things, but I don't have to be to there for a couple hours. Why don't we go back to bed for a while?"

That sounded perfect to her. She took his hand and led him back to the bedroom. They would make love, and then afterward, while he got ready for work, she would start searching his office. She wouldn't feel guilty either, because she wasn't trying to find evidence of his guilt. She was going to find the source of the two hundred thousand dollar deposit, and to whom he had wired the thirty thousand dollar payment. Because she was sure there was a reasonable explanation.

She knew deep in her heart that Jordan hadn't done anything wrong, and she was going to prove it.

Jordan sat at his desk later that morning, and though he was supposed to be working, he couldn't keep his mind off Jane. She was really getting under his skin. So much so that when he dropped her at home on his way to work, he told her he wanted to see her again that evening. They made plans to get together at his place again. He would pick her up at five and they would order in dinner and watch a movie—if he could manage to keep his hands off her for longer that ten minutes.

He tried to recall the last time he'd been so into a woman that he'd wanted to see her two nights in a row. It had been so long ago that he couldn't even remember. Nathan had lectured him about finding the right woman, and how, when he had met Ana, he just *knew*. Of course Jordan had scoffed at the idea. He told Nathan that there were so many "right women" he wouldn't know which one to choose. But after spending time with Jane, getting to know her, the idea of being with anyone else just felt…wrong.

He used to think that if he ever did decide it was time to settle down, it would take months and months for the relationship to develop. But when he kissed Jane for the first time, it felt as if something significant had happened, as though a critical part of him that he hadn't even realized was missing had shifted into place.

He shook his head and laughed at himself. A week ago if someone had even suggested such a thing were possible he would have called them crazy. And the fact that she was deceiving him and he still felt this way defied logic. But when was love ever logical? Or easy?

His phone started to ring and he found himself hoping it was Jane, but it was Nathan.

"Hey, I need a favor," Nathan said.

His first reaction was to automatically say no, because that was the way it had always been between him and Nathan. Nathan, no matter how many times Jordan had dissed him, continued to make an effort, and Jordan cut him off at every pass. But frankly, Jordan was a little tired of that game. Yeah, Nathan's meddling had made his life less than ideal, but he thought he was helping Jordan. Maybe it was time he let the past go.

Really let it go this time.

"What do you need?" he asked.

"Ana and I are supposed to go to a fundraiser tonight and our babysitter just called to say she has the flu. We called everyone else we could think of—"

"I'll watch Max," he said.

There was a pause, then he said. "Jordan?"

"Yeah."

"I was just making sure. For a second I thought I had the wrong number. I figured I would have to beg or bribe you or something."

"I love seeing Max. It sounds like fun." He was supposed to see Jane tonight, but there was no reason why she couldn't babysit with him. She could come by after Nathan and Ana left, and leave before they got home.

"You're sure?" Nathan asked.

"I'm sure."

"Because I know you're not a much of a kid person."

"What are you talking about? I love kids, and they love me."

"When was the last time you changed a diaper?"

Never, but how hard could it be? "I'm sure I can figure it out. Besides, I'll have reinforcements."

"Reinforcements?"

"I'm going to invite a friend to come by and help out."

"You're bringing a *date* to babysit?" Nathan asked. "You're joking, right?"

"She's more than just a date. She's…special."

"Special how?"

"I've been seeing this woman, and it's getting pretty

serious. And I think…" He laughed and shook his head. "I can hardly believe I'm about to say this out loud."

"You think what?"

"I think I'm falling in love with her."

For several seconds Nathan was silent, as if he was waiting for Jordan to yell *psyche!*, then he said, "Damn, you're serious."

"It's weird, I know."

"When did this happen? Is it someone I know?"

"We met a couple of months ago," he said, in part so Nathan wouldn't suspect the woman in question was Jane, and because the idea that he could fall in love with a woman after a week—especially after he'd been so adamant that he would never fall in love—seemed far-fetched even to him.

"So, when do I get to meet her?"

"Soon, I think. Maybe she'll be here tonight when you get back," he said, even though he knew she wouldn't. "So, what time do you need me there?"

"We have to be there at seven, so how about six-thirty. That will give Ana time to drill you and show you where everything is."

"Sounds good. I'll be there at six-thirty."

"See you then," he said, and before he hung up added, "And thanks, Jordan."

Jordan hung up the phone with a smile on his face. Next he dialed Jane's number. She didn't answer her home line, so he tried her cell. She answered on the first ring.

"I was just thinking about you," she said, which made him smile again. "I'm at the market and I just passed the whipped cream. I was thinking maybe we need to have another picnic in bed."

That sounded good to him, but the food play would have to wait until later.

"Slight change of plans tonight," he said, and told her about agreeing to babysit. And his plan to get her in and out undetected.

"Are you sure that's a good idea?" she asked. "What if they come home early?"

"Then we'll sneak you out the back."

"I don't know…"

"Jane, I want to see you tonight." And the night after that, and the one after that.

"Okay, but whatever time they're supposed to be home, I'm leaving an hour early."

"Fine, I'll give you the code for my front door and we can meet there after I'm done at Nathan's."

"That would work," she said, and he knew exactly what she was thinking. Being alone at his place would give her time to search for evidence, which he was sure she would have done this morning while he got ready for work, if he hadn't pulled her into the shower with him. But he had a few things he needed to take care of before he was ready to let her rifle through his personal files. Things that could be taken out of context if someone happened to stumble upon them.

He would stop home before he went to Nathan's and deal with that, then she would be free to investigate. He only hoped that she would find, or not find, what she was looking for soon, so they could start to have a normal relationship.

"I'll text you the address for Ana's condo," he said. "Be there at seven."

They hung up and Jordan forced himself to focus on work for the rest of the afternoon. He packed it in at five and went home to take care of his personal files. He gathered all the hard copies, then backed up the computer files onto a removable drive and locked it all in his office safe. Then he deleted the questionable material from his hard drive, including any emails he may have exchanged that could be misinterpreted. The idea was to give the impression that there was nothing to find, not encourage her to dig deeper.

When he was finished, it was nearly time to leave. He gave his mom a quick call to check up on her, expecting the nurse to answer, more than a little surprised when it was his dad who picked up. At first he thought he'd hit the wrong number on speed dial, but it was definitely hers.

"I was just calling to check on Mom," he said.

"She's having a really good day. She's napping now, but both the speech and physical therapists were here this morning and they say she's already making remarkable progress. She always was strong-willed."

Sure, if strong-willed was code for selfish and cold-hearted. "Dad, what's going on? What are you even doing there?"

"I'm helping."

"What happened to the baron she was so fond of?"

"I guess he showed his true colors. She needs a friend right now."

"What did she ever do to earn your friendship? I know she seems different now, but there's no guarantee she's going to stay that way."

"I'll be here for her as long as she needs me," he said.

Jordan wondered how the future Mrs. Everette number five felt about that, but he didn't ask. He just hoped his dad knew what he was doing. He may have been a real bastard when Jordan was a kid, but he'd really made an effort to change, to be not only be a better father, but a better man. Jordan hoped it didn't come back to bite him in the ass.

Thirteen

Jane hadn't been convinced that spending the evening at Nathan's place was wise, but she was glad that she'd put aside her doubts and come by. Not only was it a chance to spend time with Jordan—and get some alone time in his apartment later—watching him play with his nephew was probably one of the cutest things she'd ever seen.

Max was just under a year old with dark curly hair, big brown soulful eyes and a heart-melting dimpled grin. And he clearly adored his uncle Jordan. After a pizza dinner, which Max scarfed quite enthusiastically for someone with so few teeth, he and Jordan roughhoused on a blanket on the family room floor until eight when it was time for a diaper change and pajamas. But this time instead of wanting his uncle, he climbed into Jane's lap on the couch and snuggled up with his bottle.

"I guess he likes you," Jordan said with a grin.

She had never been much into kids. She'd never babysat

as a teen, and neither of her brothers had started families yet, so she had zero experience with them. And that line she fed Jordan about being ready to start a family was only meant to scare him away. But when Max gazed up at her with his big brown eyes she found herself thinking, *I want one of these.*

Halfway through the bottle his lids began to droop, and shortly after that he was out cold.

"Looks like he's ready for bed," Jordan said, gathering his limp little body from Jane's arms and carrying him to his crib.

While she waited Jane spread a blanket out in front of the fireplace and sat down, gazing into the fire. She hadn't expected to have this much fun tonight, nor had she expected Jordan to be such a natural with his nephew. She couldn't help wondering if he had plans to start a family someday.

Playboy that he was, she seriously doubted it, and if he did, she doubted it would be any time soon.

"Have I mentioned how sexy you look tonight?" Jordan asked from behind her.

She looked up at him and smiled. "Only about ten times."

He sat on the blanket beside her. "And I'll probably tell you ten more times."

She couldn't deny that she did look pretty good. She had taken a trip to the mall today and splurged on some new clothes. She had updated her professional wardrobe, so why not her casual clothes too? She had always assumed that skinny jeans would only accentuate her lack of figure, but the sales girl had insisted she try a pair on. They looked so good that she'd bought herself three pairs. She'd also purchased two peasant-style blouses and an emerald cashmere sweater that she was wearing now.

She looked young and hip and absolutely nothing like the drab woman she'd been the week before. She only wished she'd given herself a makeover years ago. She wished she'd had the confidence.

"So, we've got a couple of hours before you have to leave," he said. "What would you like to do now?"

"We could watch a movie."

"Or we could play a game."

"A board game?"

He grinned. "I was thinking more of a role playing game. Like, you're the teenage babysitter, and I'm your boyfriend, and you snuck me in."

She stifled a smile. "Why would I do something like that? I could get in a lot of trouble. If we got caught, they would tell my parents, and I would get grounded."

He grinned. "Because you find me completely charming and totally irresistible." He leaned close and nibbled her neck. "Besides, the element of danger is what makes it so exciting."

"Maybe I'm not that kind of girl."

"Maybe…" he said, lying back against the blanket and pulling her down beside him "…we could just make out."

It was tough to turn down an offer like that, especially when he was giving her that devilish grin. And God knows she did love kissing him.

"Just for a little while," she said, "and only kissing."

"Scout's honor," he said, but either he wasn't a very loyal scout or he wasn't a scout at all, because he had a serious case of wandering hands. At least initially, he didn't try to reach beneath her clothes, and because it felt so nice she didn't stop him. And when he slipped his hand under her sweater she figured it was above the waist, so it was okay. But when he undid the button on her jeans she put her hand over his.

"Jordan, we really shouldn't be doing this here."

"Trust me," he murmured against her lips, and when he slid the zipper down she let him. He eased his hand inside, touching her on top of her panties. In no time he had her breathing hard and arching against his hand.

"Not such a good girl anymore, are we?" he said with a wicked smile. Then he slipped his fingers past the delicate fabric. She moaned and clawed her fingers though his hair, kissing him hard as pleasure rippled through her. When it got to be too much, she grabbed his wrist to stop him. "Enough."

"Uh-uh. I want to do that again," he said, but she wanted to make him feel good too. She got up on her knees and pushed him down on to his back, then she unfastened his jeans.

He grinned and said, "Maybe I'm not that kind of boy."

Apparently he was though, because when she freed his erection from his boxers he didn't try to stop her, and when she leaned over and took him in her mouth he moaned and sank his fingers through her hair. He pushed his jeans down his hips to give her better access and within minutes she could feel him tensing. He had a special sensitive spot just below the family jewels, and when she touched him there he lost it.

"I think I like this game," he said, grinning up at her.

Her too, but it was time they act like responsible babysitters and behaved themselves.

Nathan and his fiancée weren't due back for several hours, so they straightened themselves up, laid down together on the couch and switched on the television. But apparently there had been some sort of change of plans because less than half an hour later the door opened and Nathan and Ana walked in.

* * *

Jane sat at her desk Monday morning, one eye on her computer screen, the other on the phone. She wasn't sure why she was so worried, since technically she hadn't done anything wrong. Nathan knew that the investigation would necessitate her getting close to Jordan. Hell, hadn't he been the one to call her into his office and give her advice on how to keep Jordan *interested?* Well, he was, so she shouldn't feel guilty for doing exactly what Nathan had told her to. Right?

The problem was, when she and Jordan were putting on their coats that night, and Jordan's back was turned, Nathan had given her this *look.* She couldn't help feeling that in his eyes, she had done something immoral. Which technically she had, but as far as she could tell, he didn't know that she'd slept with Jordan. Unless Jordan had confided in him, not realizing that this information would be enough to get her fired on the spot. But Jordan didn't seem the type to kiss and tell.

The fact that Jordan had left for the refinery at least a half an hour ago, and Nathan hadn't summoned her to his office was a good sign, right?

Someone walked into the office and she looked up from her screen to find the Mr. Everette in question looming over her, looking none too happy.

Oh hell.

"Is he here?"

She shook her head, hoping he came to talk to his brother and not her. "He'll be at the refinery most of the day."

"In his office," Nathan said, jerking his head in that direction. "Now."

Oh, this was not good. She got up and walked into

Jordan's office and Nathan followed her in, closing the door behind them.

"This has got to end," he said. "You need to get the information you came here for and get out before this thing you have going with my brother goes any further."

Okay, so he clearly knew something was going on, and he believed that if it wasn't sexual, it would be soon.

"I know how that probably looked the other night, but as I told you before, the investigation would necessitate a certain level of intima—"

"He's falling in love with you."

She blinked. "What? No, he's not…that's ridiculous. Jordan doesn't do love. He doesn't even get tied down."

"Apparently he does now."

She shook her head. "No, that's not possible. You've got it all wrong. It probably just looks—"

"Jane, he *told* me."

No way. "He actually told you that he's in love with *me?*"

"He told me that he's been seeing a woman, and that he's falling in love with her, and he was going to have her come over while he babysat. So unless there was some other woman with you guys at my place, he had to be talking about you."

Suddenly her heart was beating so fast she could hardly breathe. Could it be possible that Jordan really did love her?

"You're sleeping with him," Nathan said.

Jane bit her lip. She could deny it, but hadn't she lied enough? And when he learned the truth, wouldn't it just make things worse?

He sighed and shook his head. "Look, I know how persuasive my brother can be, but seriously, I thought you would have the professional ethics, not to mention the good sense, to know when to draw the line."

He was right. There was no excusing her behavior. But in her own defense, never in her wildest dreams had she imagined that Jordan would fall for her. And the fact that she was falling for him too was beside the point, because the minute he found out that she'd been lying to him all this time, that would be the end of it. She knew that for a fact because if the tables were turned, she didn't think she could ever forgive that kind of deception. "I take full responsibility for my actions," she said.

"I could have you fired for this," he said.

Yes, he could, and she would deserve it. But she was so close to wrapping up this investigation. "I have access to his home office. To his files and his computer. I just need a little more time."

"Find what you need and end this thing."

"I will." Phew, that was a close one.

He pulled the door open and started to leave.

"Nathan, wait."

Hand on the knob, he turned back to her.

"For what it's worth, I really care about Jordan. I could love him." Could? Hell, who was she kidding? She already did.

"But?"

"But I know that once he learns the truth…" She shrugged, not even sure why she was telling Nathan this. "It's going to be over. He would never be able to trust me again."

"For good reason," Nathan said, twisting the knife a little deeper. But she deserved it.

Nathan left and Jane tried to concentrate on work, but her mind kept wandering. Nathan was right. She needed to get this investigation wrapped up. The twenty minutes she'd spent in his home office after he'd gone to sleep Saturday night, and while he was in the shower Sunday morning, hadn't been close to adequate. There were just too many papers to go through, and she needed more time to copy the files off his hard drive, even though she was convinced she wouldn't find anything. She knew Jordan hadn't done anything wrong.

Her cell phone rang and though she half expected it to be Jordan, it was her sister, Mary.

"We need to talk," she said. "Are you busy tonight?"

"Actually, I am." She was meeting Jordan at his place after work for another "picnic" in bed.

"This really can't wait," she said, sounding almost desperate. And Mary didn't do desperate.

"We could meet for a drink at twelve-thirty," Jane said.

"That'll work."

They agreed on a place, and when Jane arrived her sister was already there, nursing an apple martini.

She stood and hugged Jane when she reached the table, which in itself was sort of weird, but when she said, "Oh my gosh, you look fantastic!" Jane knew something was up.

She took off her coat and sat down. "Okay, what do you want?"

Mary feigned an innocent look. "What do you mean?"

"The only time you're nice to me is when you want something from me."

"That's not true."

Jane glared at her.

"Okay, maybe it is a *little* true."

The waiter stopped by the table and Jane ordered a Manhattan. When he was gone she pulled Mary's business card from her purse where she'd stuffed it Friday night. "You can have this back."

Mary actually blushed as she took it. "I take it you guys aren't just *friends*."

"It doesn't matter. It was a rotten thing to do."

She stuck the card in her purse. "You're right. I just thought…" she shrugged. "I don't know what I thought. But his name sounded really familiar, so I looked him up on Google."

Uh oh.

"COO of an oil company, huh? The guy is a *billionaire*. How'd you swing that one?"

She folded her arms. "Because clearly a man like him would never go for a dog like me."

Mary blinked. "That isn't what I meant. I've always thought you were pretty, you just never seemed to try very hard to look…nicer."

Years of resentment suddenly welled up and threatened to choke her. "Maybe because every time I tried, I was shut down. Everyone made me believe I was destined to be Plain Jane forever."

Mary looked genuinely confused. "When did anyone ever do that?"

"It was constant. Like when I tried your makeup and you laughed at me."

"Of course I laughed at you. You looked like a cheap hooker."

"Did you ever think to show me the right way to do it?"

"Why? So you could be smarter *and* prettier than me?"

Jane drew back in her chair, feeling as if she'd been slapped. *"What?"*

"You don't like the way you've been treated, Jane? Well, boo hoo. Do you have any clue how hard I've had to work to keep up with you? How many times I had to listen to Mom and Dad bragging about your vast accomplishments to people. And 'Mary, oh, she's the *pretty* one,' like I was some idiot they kept around because they felt sorry for me."

Jane had no idea her sister felt that way. Mary always seemed so confident in the fact that she was better than everyone else.

The waiter deposited Jane's drink and the bill at the table. She took a sip then told her sister, "You aren't an idiot. Idiots are not accepted into law school."

"No, but do you think I like knowing that you're always going to be a better lawyer than me, even though you've never applied yourself?"

"Never *applied* myself?" Was she kidding? "I was never given the chance. I got stuck in the back doing everyone else's grunt work."

"Oh, poor Jane. I am so *sick* of that self-righteous bull. When did you show even an ounce of motivation to do more? Do you think the rest of us built a client base by just sitting back and letting cases fall in our laps? We've all worked damned hard building our careers. What makes you think you deserve special treatment? A higher GPA? Well, I hate to break it to you, baby sister, but that's not the way it works in the real world."

Jane didn't know what to say. Maybe she could have been more aggressive. Maybe, because school had come so easy to her, she expected the same in her career? And now that she thought about it, was it any different at Edwin Associates? If the undercover position hadn't literally fallen into her lap, would she have spent years feeling unappreciated, and passed over when it was no one's fault but her own? "I guess I've just always felt that you guys were trying to hold me back."

"The only one holding you back is *you*. Not that I'm complaining. It worked out great for me. All your hard work made me look good."

"And now that I'm gone?"

Mary leaned forward, imploring her, "Please come back."

The sudden plea surprised her. She'd been taunted and badgered about leaving the practice, she'd been made to feel she was an outcast, but never once had anyone asked her to come back.

"Mom and Dad are too proud to say so, but they miss you, and they *need* you there. We all do."

She scoffed. "I seriously doubt that."

Mary shook her head. "See, there you go underestimating yourself again."

She was right.

"If this was some sort of protest against the family, hasn't it gone on long enough?"

"It wasn't like that. I just wanted to try something... different. I felt underappreciated."

"They appreciate you. Believe me. Even if they don't know how to express it. And they're driving *me* crazy!"

"Better you than me."

"You should come back. Unless you're really happy in your *new* job," Mary said. "Which, by the way, I know for a fact is *not* at Anderson Tech. I have a friend from college who works there."

Damn. If she had known that, she would have picked a different company. "You didn't tell anyone?"

She shrugged. "I figured if you were going to lie, you had a pretty good reason."

"I would have told Mom and Dad the truth, but I knew they would be upset, and it wouldn't be worth the hassle. They would just tell me I'm wasting my law degree."

"What are you doing?"

"Something they definitely wouldn't approve of."

Mary gasped and said in a hushed voice, "Are you a *stripper?*"

Jane laughed. "Of course not! Why would even you think that?"

"Well, there's your new *look* and you definitely have the body for it."

"Are you forgetting that I'm slightly lacking in the breast department?"

"You're proportional. Besides, a lot of men go for that look."

"Well, I'm not a stripper. It's nothing that racy."

Mary leaned in closer. "So what is it?"

She wondered if she could trust her sister with the truth. "You have to swear not to tell anyone. Not Mom and Dad, or the boys. And especially not Jordan."

She looked puzzled. "He doesn't know where you work?"

"You have to *promise*."

"*Okay,* I won't tell a soul, I promise."

She told Mary about Edwin Associates, and that she was on her first undercover assignment.

"Not racy! Oh my God, are you kidding? That is so cool." She laughed and shook her head. "I am, like, so completely impressed right now. It must be so exciting."

Exciting? Maybe it should have been, but in reality the lying made her stomach knot and the sneaking around gave her anxiety. Yes, it was only her first assignment, but she was beginning to believe that she just didn't possess the killer instinct.

If she was being totally honest with herself, the only thing she really enjoyed about the job was spending time with Jordan.

"Mary, I hate it."

"What? Why?"

"I was going crazy cooped up in that dinky little cubicle

they put me in. I wanted to be out in the field, where the excitement is, but the truth is, I'm not any good at it."

"I find that really hard to believe. You excel at everything you do. You always have."

"I fell in love with the man I'm supposed to be investigating."

Her mouth fell open. "Oh my God, are you investigating *Jordan Everette?*"

"Shh! Keep your voice down."

Mary slapped a hand over her mouth. "Sorry!"

Jane leaned in closer and said quietly, "I've been working as a temp secretary in his office."

"And things got hot and steamy? Sounds like a porno movie."

Jane laughed and kicked her under the table. "We've never done anything at work. And it wasn't like I went after him. He pursued me."

"I'm not surprised. Clearly the man has it bad for you. The way he was looking at you the other night...*wow.* I can't even remember the last time a man looked at me that way. I always knew you could do better than Drake the snake."

"Drake the *what?*"

"Drake the snake. That's what the family has been calling him since he left you for Megan."

"He did me a favor."

"Obviously, because now you're in love with a man who's rich and powerful and *gorgeous,* who seems to worship the ground you walk on."

"And who is going to hate my guts when he learns who I really am."

"Hmm, that could be a problem. Not to mention that you're still investigating him, right? For all you know he may be guilty."

She shook her head. "No, if you knew him, you would know he isn't capable of hurting anyone."

"Because after a week you know him that well? Sounds like maybe you're not being objective."

Mary was right. Without a shred of proof she already had him exonerated. "As I said, I suck at this."

"So quit."

"I can't."

"If you don't like it, why not?"

Because the minute she did, it was going to be over for her and Jordan. He would learn the truth. "I'm just not ready to give up yet."

"What you mean is, you're not ready to give *him* up."

Exactly. The longer she dragged this out, the longer she could be with Jordan.

And the more it would hurt when it was over.

Fourteen

Despite the doctor's warning that she might never talk normally again, in the three weeks since her stroke, Jordan's mom had been defying the odds. Though he and Nathan had both feared that the embarrassment of having an impediment would hamper her recovery, and maybe cause her to hide herself away, they couldn't have been more wrong. She had welcomed visits from her friends and held her head high when her speech necessitated her repeating things to be understood. Only ten days after her discharge she returned to her bridge club and even attended a charity luncheon.

Even more remarkable was the way the stroke had changed her. Jordan didn't know if it was the damage to her brain, or simply the realization that she wasn't invincible, and life was precious, but she suddenly seemed to realize how important her family was to her. She welcomed visits from her sons and Nathan had even begun bringing Ana and Max to see her. For someone who had no interest in her own children, she was turning out to be a doting grandmother.

But the weirdest thing by far was her relationship with Jordan's dad. He'd been spending an excessive amount of time at her place. So excessive that his fiancée packed her things and moved back to Seattle. Jordan had never heard his parents utter so much as a single kind word to each other, but now it seemed that they had finally connected. Jordan wasn't sure if it would last, but for his father's sake he hoped so.

And then there was Jane. Despite nearing the three week mark, when normally he would begin to get bored with a woman—especially one he was spending nearly every waking moment with, he found her more intriguing and more desirable every day.

He wished her part of the investigation would finally close so that they could have a normal relationship. He wanted to take her out in public, do the normal things that couples do. A nice dinner and a trip to the theater or even just burgers and a movie. She was fanatical about them not being seen together in anything other than a professional capacity. He was getting tired of the sneaking around.

What he didn't get was, what was taking so long? He knew for a fact that she'd had more than adequate opportunity to search both his office at work and at home. He made sure that she had access to his computer and all but a select few of his financial files. There wasn't much about him that she didn't know, or have access to, yet they were still playing this game and there seemed to be no end in sight.

There was one thing he was going to miss when she was done though. Jane was an awesome secretary. In some ways even better than Tiffany. And God knows he'd kept her busy. With an equipment upgrade happening in just two days, followed by a vigorous safety inspection, Jordan had been spending more and more time at the refinery. It was during the last upgrade that the sabotage occurred, and tensions were high both at the refinery and the corporate office. As COO, the responsibility of keeping the men safe fell almost entirely on Jordan. This time before they brought the equipment back online, he planned to personally inspect every inch of the line.

The Friday before the scheduled maintenance, he was going over a few last minute changes to the schedule when Jane buzzed him.

"You have a call on line one from a Peter Burke."

Jordan tensed. Peter Burke was a manager at the refinery. However, Jordan suspected that his call had nothing to do with a work matter. They had discussed this and Peter knew better than to call Jordan at the office regarding personal matters.

"I've got it," he told Jane. "And could you please close my door?"

"Of course." She disconnected and appeared in his office doorway. She flashed him a smile, then closed the door.

He took a deep breath, then picked up line one. "Peter, what the hell are you doing calling me here?"

"I've tried you at home and on your cell. I've left you messages. I can't talk to you at the refinery."

"I would have gotten back to you when I had the time."

"Jordan, I'm desperate."

"I told you that I would get you the money and I will."

"But if I don't get it soon—"

"Now just isn't a good time. With the upgrade next week *everyone* is under scrutiny. Especially the refinery workers."

He cursed under his breath. "I'm sorry, Jordan. Maybe I should just come clean, tell everyone the truth."

"And risk losing your job, and your family?"

"Considering what I've done, maybe they would be better off without me. If I don't get the money soon, it might be out of my hands."

He closed his eyes and sighed. It was emotional blackmail. He never should have let himself get pulled into this mess. "Look, I have about half in cash in my safe at home. Will that be enough to hold you until I can get my hands on the rest?"

"That would be great," he said sounding relieved.

"This time, I want you to get some help, Peter."

"I will. I promise. I won't screw this up again."

"I'll get the money together and call you with a meeting place."

"Thanks, Jordan. I owe you."

He certainly did. But this was the last time.

He grabbed his coat and headed out of his office, wondering for a fleeting moment if Jane could have been listening in on his phone conversation, but she was at her desk, talking on her cell phone. She looked up at him and smiled. "Mary, I have to let you go. I'll call you later." She hung up and said, "Sorry about that."

"Your sister?"

"Yeah, she was giving me another lecture on the virtues of coming back to work for my parents."

She had been weighing the pros and cons of going back to the family practice for a couple of weeks now. Personally, he thought it was an excellent idea. "Still haven't made up your mind?"

"I'll probably do it, if for no other reason than I'm running out of money." She grinned. "I guess I sort of like making her beg."

He laughed. She was starting to sound more and more like him all the time. But he was glad she was patching things up with her family. It seemed they were both doing a bit of that lately.

"You're leaving for the refinery already?" she asked.

"Yeah, I have a stop to make on the way there. Do you have that equipment list I asked for?"

"Right here," she said, grabbing the folder from the corner of her desk and handing it to him. "Are we still on for tonight?"

"Absolutely. Do you want to cook or pick something up?"

"I doubt I'll be done here before six, then I have to go home and change, and I would have to stop at the market—"

"Takeout it is. Unless you want to go to a restaurant somewhere." At her exasperated look he shrugged and said, "It was just an idea."

"I'll see you tonight." She smiled up at him. She looked like her normal self, but when he looked deeper there was something in her eyes…what if she had been listening? She could have taken what he said completely out of context. But she knew him, and she had to know by now that he was one of the good guys, that he wouldn't deliberately do anything to hurt anyone. She had to care about him as much as he cared for her.

He had this burning need, this sudden desire to hear her say the words.

"Come here." He took her hand and pulled her up out of her chair, leading her into his office and shutting the door.

"Jordan, what are you—" She let out a soft gasp as he pulled her into his arms, and when he kissed her, she melted against him.

He gazed down at her, cupping her face in his hands. "I love you, Jane. I've never said that to a woman. But I need you to know how much you mean to me."

She smiled up at him. "I love you too, Jordan."

He closed his eyes and pressed his forehead to hers. He never imagined that hearing those words would feel so good. So why, as he kissed her goodbye and walked out, did he have the sinking feeling that something just wasn't right?

Maybe his guilty conscience was finally getting the best of him.

Jane sat at her desk, replaying Jordan's conversation on the mini digital recorder, trying to come up with some logical explanation for what was said, feeling sick all the way down to her soul because she knew what she had to do.

She had been so certain that he was innocent, that he would never do anything to hurt anyone. She still couldn't wrap her head around it, couldn't make herself believe it. Whether or not he was actually paying this Peter Burke person a bribe to tamper with equipment, she couldn't sit back and do nothing. If she didn't report this, and there was another explosion, if people were hurt because she had proof but did nothing, she would never be able to live with herself.

Jordan's sudden declaration of love wasn't making this any easier. It was almost as if he knew who she was, knew she was listening, and suspected that she would turn him in. Maybe he thought that telling her he loved her would change her mind.

But how could he know? Wouldn't he have said something?

Though she had strict instructions to take all new

information directly to her boss at Edwin Associates, she just couldn't do it. She palmed the mini recorder and walked down the hall to Mr. Blair's office, hands trembling, heart beating so hard her chest ached.

She must have looked as bad as she felt. When Bren saw her, she frowned and said, "Honey are you okay?"

Come on Jane, pull it together, be a professional.

"I need to see him," she told Bren. "It's urgent."

She picked up the phone and buzzed her boss, relaying the message, then she told Jane, "Go on in."

Swallowing back her distress, and squaring her shoulders, she walked into Adam Blaire's office.

He rose from his seat, "Miss Monroe."

"I have something I need you to listen to." She pressed Play and handed him the digital recorder.

He sat back down, stone-faced as he listened to the entire conversation. When it was over he hit Stop, then muttered a curse that she didn't think men as polished as him uttered in mixed company. Then he looked up at her and said, "Sorry."

"It's okay."

"Has anyone else heard this?"

She shook her head. "I thought it would be best if I gave it to you first."

"You did the right thing. Where is he now?"

"On his way to the refinery."

He picked up the phone and dialed his secretary. "Get Jordan back here immediately. Tell him to come straight to my office. It's urgent." He hung up and gestured to the chair across from his desk. "Have a seat, Miss Monroe."

He wanted her to *stay?* The information she'd gathered was quite possibly about to ruin Jordan's career, *his life,* and Mr. Blair wanted her to watch? She knew there were people who relished this moment, took personal and professional pride in bringing down the bad guys, but she felt like garbage.

Jordan had told her he loved her, and she had betrayed him.

God, she hated this job, and the second she was out of here, she was going back to the office and submitting her resignation. After that she was going to see her parents, and she would *beg* for her old job back if she had to. She would rather work in a fast-food burger joint earning minimum wage than put herself through this again.

"Miss Monroe?"

She looked up and realized Mr. Blair was watching her. "Huh?"

"Are you okay?"

Other than the fact that she felt like she might be sick? "I'm fine. I just…"

"You like him."

Was she that transparent? She bit her lip and nodded. "He's just so…so…"

"Charming? Personable?"

Not to mention sweet and sexy and generous and kind. "I didn't expect to find evidence against him."

"There's still a chance that there's a reasonable explanation."

He didn't believe that, and neither did she.

"You two have become…close?" he asked.

She no longer had to worry about her career as an investigator. It was over. She didn't see any point in lying to him. Besides, when Jordan walked in and saw her there, he was going to be furious. Adam would have to be a moron not to realize that something had happened. And he was no moron.

She nodded. "I didn't mean for it to happen."

He smiled, which he didn't seem to do very often. "We never do, do we?"

"I can't do this again. I'm going back to the law."

His brows rose. "You're a lawyer?"

She nodded. "I left our family practice and started working at Edwin Associates six months ago. This was my first undercover assignment."

"For what it's worth, I never would have guessed. You gave the impression of being a seasoned professional. And if you're looking for a job, I'm sure we can find a place for you in our law department."

"I appreciate that," she said, but once she left today, she would never set foot in the Western Oil corporate headquarters ever again. It would be too awkward.

The door opened and Jordan walked in, still wearing his coat, and Jane's heart sank to her toes.

"You wanted to see me," he said.

Mr. Blair stood, and motioned Jane to come stand to the side of him. "That was awfully quick."

"I hadn't left yet. I was grabbing a sandwich in the coffee shop to eat on the way."

Jane waited for him to ask what she was doing there, for surprise or confusion. For *something*. But he didn't even look at her.

Why didn't he look at her?

"Why don't you have a seat."

He folded his arms. "I get the feeling I'm about to face the firing squad, so I think I'd rather stand."

Mr. Blair pressed Play on the recorder and set it on his desk. After about three seconds, Jordan said, "I recall the conversation, considering it took place, oh, about twenty minutes ago."

Adam stopped the recording. "If you haven't already

figured it out, Miss Monroe isn't a temp. She's an undercover investigator for Edwin Associates."

Jane waited for the anger, for the disdain, but still, nothing. Didn't he care that she'd been lying to him? That he'd told her he loved her not twenty minutes ago and she had ratted him out?

There was only one logical explanation, one that made her blood go cold. He already knew. He had known from the start, and all this time he had just been screwing with her. To what? Throw her off the scent, so she wouldn't learn the truth?

Some investigator she'd turned out to be. She'd been played and she hadn't had a clue.

"I know how the conversation sounds," Jordan told Mr. Blair. "But it isn't what you think."

"So tell me what it is."

Jordan nodded in her direction. "She has to go."

She. That's all she was now? One minute he was telling her he loved her, now they weren't even on a first name basis?

Humiliation burned her cheeks, drove a spike through her heart. How could she have been so stupid? How could she have believed that someone like him would truly care about someone like her? It was all a game to him.

"She brought this recording directly to me instead of reporting to her boss," Mr. Blair said. "And there's nothing stopping her from doing it now, so I think you owe her an explanation too."

"What I'm going to tell you can't leave this room."

"I'll make that determination after I hear what you have to say."

He stepped forward, putting his hands on Adam's desk and leaning in. "No, you have to swear. Or I turn and walk, the consequences be damned."

That surprised her, and Mr. Blair too. He nodded and said, "Okay, it doesn't leave this room."

Jordan backed away from Adam's desk. "Peter Burke is a manager at the refinery."

"I know. He's the one who lost his wife last year."

Jordan nodded. "Ovarian cancer. He's raising their four kids alone. Even with health insurance the medical bills wiped him out. He was on the brink of bankruptcy, about to lose his home. He's a good guy, a loyal employee. I felt sorry for him and I offered to help. And for obvious reasons I wanted it kept confidential."

"Or every employee with a down-on-his-luck story would be hounding you," Adam said.

"Exactly. I figured I would give him the money, he would get back on his feet and everything would be cool. But it wasn't. His wife's death hit him harder than anyone realized. He started drinking, and gambling, then he started missing work, screwing up on the job. We tried to cut him slack, tried to get him help. Then he came to me a few months ago, just before the explosion. He got himself in deep with a loan shark and they were threatening him, threatening to hurt his kids. He was desperate."

"Let me guess, he owed them thirty thousand dollars," Adam said.

Jordan narrowed his eyes at him. "You knew?"

"Only that you received a wire from an offshore account for two hundred thousand, and wired thirty back out."

"From *my* offshore account," Jordan said. "Most of my money is tied up in investments. When I need cash I dip into my other accounts."

"So I assume he's asking for money again?" Mr. Blair said.

"He's in bad shape. He was supposed to join Alcoholics Anonymous. I even found him a sponsor, but he stopped going after a couple of meetings. He's back in deep with the loan sharks and now his sister-in-law is trying to take his children. Those kids are all he has left. I don't know what he'll do if he loses them."

"So why the secrecy?"

"The fewer people who know about this, the better. His sister-in-law has already filed to get custody."

"And her lawyer will be talking to all his coworkers," Jane said. If the sister-in-law had a good lawyer, and she probably did, his work would be the first place they would look for dirt.

"People are already being subpoenaed," Jordan told her, then he turned back to Adam. "And there's another reason I wanted to keep this from you. A selfish reason."

"I'm listening."

He took a deep breath and blew it out, as if what he was about to say was a struggle for him. "Though I didn't tamper with the equipment, or directly cause the explosion, I'm responsible."

Fifteen

Jordan had been holding that in for so long, carrying the guilt, it was a relief to finally let it out. And he could thank Jane for that. At first he'd been pissed that she'd ratted him out, especially after claiming to love him. But she had done him a favor. She had stopped this before it completely spiraled out of control.

"How are you responsible?" Adam asked.

"I knew Peter was having a rough time. He'd just quit drinking and the pressure was high. Whoever tampered with the equipment clearly knew it too, because it happened in Peter's section."

Adam sat back in his chair. "You think he missed something."

Jordan nodded. "I do. Knowing what a mess he was, I never should have allowed him to be a part of the safety inspection. I should have called someone else in, but he insisted he could handle it."

"Jordan, had you considered that he could be the one who tampered with the equipment?"

"Considered and dismissed it. He's a good guy. Besides, what reason could he have had to do it? I was giving him the money he needed."

Adam got a thoughtful expression on his face. "Maybe you did cut him too much slack, but you had no way of knowing that someone was planning to tamper with the equipment. Had it not been for that, things could have gone smoothly."

"But it happened, and it's about time I take responsibility for my part."

"It was a judgment call. A bad one maybe, but there was no malicious intent. But something is going to have to be done about Peter."

"I know. Anyone else would have fired him months ago. Maybe I should have."

"I don't want to tell you what to do, but sometimes you have to let a person hit rock bottom before they can learn to help themselves."

He honestly thought he could help Peter, that he would listen. Up until now, Jordan had always considered his arrogance an asset, but he had screwed up this time. Thought he was above reproach.

He glanced up at Jane. She stood there taking it all in. He could only imagine what she was thinking. And he knew he couldn't keep lying to her. He owed her and Adam the entire truth.

"There's something else I have to tell you," Jordan told Adam. "I knew Jane was an investigator."

"How long?" Adam asked.

He looked at Jane. "From the first day."

Adam shook his head. "Christ, Jordan. Why? Why

didn't you say something? Why go along with it, wasting everyone's time?"

He had a whole list of excuses, but there was really one reason. "Because I was pissed, and stupid. And arrogant enough to think that I could have a little fun at everyone else's expense."

"Excuse me," Jane said, her face pale, looking like she might be sick, walking past him to the door.

"Jane!" he called after her, but she slammed it shut behind her. He cursed. If she would have just let him finish. "Are we through here?" he asked Adam.

Adam's laugh was a wry one. "Not even close, but what I have to say can wait. From the looks of it, you have bigger problems."

He was right about that, because at this moment, the only thing in his life that really mattered was Jane.

By the time he caught up with her she was gathering the few personal items she had on her desk and shoving them into her purse.

"We need to talk," he told her. "You didn't let me finish."

She didn't even look at him. "What's left to say? You played me. You were just having fun at my expense."

"Only at first."

"You know. I should have realized. I mean, someone like you being attracted to someone like me? How ridiculous is that?"

"Not ridiculous at all."

"I've got to hand it to you though, you had me snowed. And everyone else apparently."

"I never once lied about the way I feel about you, Jane."

She turned to him. "Forgive me if I don't believe you."

"You weren't exactly honest either."

"I'm sorry that I lied to you, Jordan, but I was doing my

job. And not very well apparently, because not a day went by that I wasn't sick with guilt for not telling you the truth. I fell hard for you, knowing that the minute you learned my real identity you would probably never want to see me again."

"And you thought you would improve your chances by turning me in?"

"What if I didn't and something had happened? What if more people had been hurt?"

"You didn't trust me."

"You will never know how hard it was for me to give him that recording. But you're right, I guess I didn't trust you. Which is why I think we should end this right now."

"Jane." He reached for her and she jerked her arm away.

"Just tell me this," she said. "If it hadn't been for what happened today, would you have ever told me the truth?"

"The point is that I *did* tell you."

She looked so…disappointed. "No, that's not the point, not at all." She grabbed her purse and her coat, turned to him and said, "Goodbye, Jordan."

And idiot that he was, he didn't even try to go after her.

"We found him."

Jordan looked up from his monitor to find Adam leaning in his office doorway later that evening, looking smug.

"Found who?"

"The saboteur."

His heart dropped. "Are you serious?"

"Only he isn't."

Yeah, it had been a really long day, but Jordan was coherent enough to realize that Adam wasn't making sense. "I'm not following you."

He crossed the room. "After our talk today, I got to

thinking. Call it a hunch, but I called Edwin Associates and told them to bring Peter Burke in for questioning."

"Adam, you promised—"

"I told them to tell Peter that we'd caught the man responsible for the sabotage, and that it was you."

"Me?"

"He cracked in ten seconds flat."

Jordan suddenly felt sick to his stomach. "It was Peter?"

"Peter caused the explosion, but it wasn't sabotage."

"Are you saying it was an *accident*?"

"It was a few minutes before that section was supposed to come back online and he noticed a faulty gauge. Instead of calling in a maintenance crew and delaying things another day, he thought he could adjust it himself. And maybe he could have if he hadn't been half in the bag at the time."

"So, all this time we thought it was deliberate, and it was really just an accident?" He shook his head. "Unbelievable."

"I think the guilt was getting to him. He was ready to confess."

"How did you even know to question him?"

He shrugged. "Like I said, it was a hunch."

Everyone had been so convinced it had been deliberate, no one had even considered that it was just a stupid mistake. "This is my fault," Jordan said. "In my attempt to help Peter, I only made things worse."

"Yes, you did."

"And you should be asking for my resignation."

"I should, yes."

"But…?"

"When I consider all the good that you've done for the company, it only seems fair to give you another chance. But I will be watching you."

He didn't have to ask to know that he'd lost any chance at the CEO position. He'd been so sure he was infallible, he'd gotten cocky. He had done this to himself.

"So, what happens to Peter now?" Jordan asked.

"Suspension. Only after he completes a rehab program will he even be considered for reassignment."

"You didn't have to do that. You could have just fired him."

"I could have, but you vouched for his character, and I trust you. If you say he's a good guy, I believe you."

"And if he screws this up?"

He shrugged. "At least we tried."

"So, with the mystery solved, I guess that means you can retire now."

"That's the plan. With any luck I'll be out of here by the end of the month, which will give me a full month and a half with Katy before the baby is due."

"Then what? Stay-at-home dad?"

Adam grinned. "Actually, Katy's family owns a ranch, and since we own the adjacent land, I was thinking I may just give ranching a try."

"I guess that means your replacement will be announced soon."

"The board meets Monday to appoint my successor."

Jordan already knew that it wasn't going to be him, not after today. Which seriously sucked, but he'd done this to himself. He thought he was invincible. That the rules didn't apply to him.

"I noticed that Miss Monroe is gone," Adam said.

"HR is putting in for a replacement. Someone should be here tomorrow morning."

"Did you and she work things out?"

"If by working it out you mean her saying it's over and leaving in a huff, then, yeah."

"Maybe this is a stupid question, but did you say you were sorry?"

"Of course I did." Hadn't he? "She seems to be pretty clear about what she wants. Or doesn't want. Besides, it's better this way," he said, knowing the second the words left his mouth that they weren't true. But it was out of his hands. He couldn't force her to love him, to forgive him. "When it comes to relationships the only thing I'm really good at is keeping them superficial and short."

"Well, if you change your mind, there's always groveling."

That wasn't going to happen. He had tried to reason with her, tried to work it out. The ball was in her court now.

The board's choice was announced Monday afternoon. As of March 1, Emilio Suarez would be appointed CEO of Western Oil. Nathan's relationship with Ana killed his chances, and Jordan didn't have to ask why he was passed over. Emilio had worked hard to become who he was, and he deserved the position. And though Jordan was disappointed, he was okay with it. Odd considering just a week ago he had been wholly convinced the spot was his. A lot had changed since then.

He had changed.

After Jordan returned from the refinery, Nathan stopped by his office. "Got a minute?"

"Come on in." It was only six, but he felt as if he'd worked a twenty-hour day.

"I heard that the update at the refinery went off without a hitch."

"Yep. We're running at full capacity."

"So…I guess you heard that Emilio got the job."

Jordan nodded. "Yep."

"I thought you should know that I turned in my

resignation. I'm leaving Western Oil. Word is going to get around quickly and I wanted to be the one to tell you."

He should have seen this coming. "Just because you didn't make CEO, you're going to quit?"

"That's only part of the reason. You and I both know, now that I'm connected to the Birch family, it's only a matter of time before they push me out. Ana's father wants me to come work for him. He made me an offer I just couldn't refuse."

Jordan didn't have the energy to be angry. Nor did he know why he should be. He should be happy for Nathan, yet in a way he felt as if he was being abandoned. He didn't like change, and with both Adam and Nathan leaving, and Emilio as CEO, Jordan had the feeling that things would be very different. But he forced a smile and said, "That's great. You deserve it."

"I was afraid you might be upset."

"Because I'm that much of an arrogant jerk?"

"Sometimes."

Yeah, he deserved that.

"You know, if you ever decide you want to leave Western, I'm sure I can pull some strings…"

Jordan's main motivation for working at Western had been the need to prove that he was better than Nathan. To get out from under his brother's shadow. In hindsight the whole thing seemed childish. And the real pisser was that despite what a jerk Jordan had been, and continued to be, Nathan was still looking out for him. He was a good brother. And clearly the better man. And though it might be easier to start over somewhere new, he needed to face what he'd done and make amends.

"I appreciate the offer," he told Nathan. "But I'm content where I am. I like my job, and the people I work with."

"Well, if you ever change your mind…"

"You'll be the first to know."

"By the way, the wedding is next weekend and you still haven't RSVP'd. Will you be bringing a date or going stag?"

Why did he get the feeling that Nathan wasn't asking just to confirm his attendance at the wedding. "It's over."

"I thought you loved her."

"I can't make her love me."

"I was under the impression that she already does."

"She lied to me."

"And you lied to her." At Jordan's surprised look, he added, "Adam told me that you knew who she was all along and didn't say anything. Dumb-ass move."

"There's a first for everything."

Nathan laughed and shook his head. "Well, at least you still have your ego."

"I apologized, she walked out the door. The ball is in her court now."

Nathan shot him a disbelieving look. "*You* apologized. You actually said, 'Jane, I'm sorry.'"

Well, he thought he had, but when he replayed the conversation back in his head, he realized he hadn't actually said the words. "There was an implied apology."

"How's the view from up there, Jordan?"

He frowned. "Up where?"

"Your moral high horse."

Jordan rubbed his hands over his face. Nathan was right of course. He was being an idiot. But only because he didn't know what else to do. "My longest relationship before now was less than six months. Even if I wanted to make this work, I don't have a clue how."

"You'll figure it out."

"How?"

"You could start by telling her how you feel. And I suggest a real apology this time."

"And if that doesn't work?"

He shrugged. "You beg?"

"And if she still says no?"

A slow smile crept across his face. "You're scared. You're afraid of being rejected."

Damn right he was. He was Jordan Everette, billionaire. Ladies' man. Women chased him, not the other way around. But Jane, she was playing by an entirely different set of rules. She didn't want Jordan the billionaire, she wanted the man who, until recently, he'd kept locked up inside. She was the only woman who had ever really seen him.

"I don't have to tell you that this sort of thing doesn't happen every day," Nathan said. "You take the risk."

That was Nathan, still looking out for him. But this time Jordan didn't mind. Because Nathan was right.

Jordan pushed himself up from his chair and told his brother, "You've got a point."

"I do?"

Jordan laughed. "Yeah, and I have to go."

Sixteen

Jane was still at work Monday evening when her sister stopped by her new office.

"It's after eight. What are you still doing here?"

"I was just going over a few of our active cases, bringing myself up to date."

"So, how does it feel to be back?"

Last Friday after she'd left Western Oil, Jane swallowed her pride and went to see her parents. When she told them she'd just quit her job, they all but begged her to come back. She had insisted that this time things would have to be different. She wouldn't let herself fall back into the rut of doing everyone's grunt work. She planned to take charge of her career, build a client base. They promised to help make that happen. And on top of everything else, she even managed to negotiate a better salary. Then the family took her out to dinner to celebrate. They were happy to have her back, and it was good to be back, to feel as if she were in charge of her life again.

"Good," she told her sister. "It's nice to be doing a job I know I don't suck at."

"So…have you talked to him?"

Jane didn't have to ask who she meant. Jordan was all she had been able to think about. And she missed him. She missed their dinners in bed and the way he teased her. She missed the way she felt when she was with him, as if she were the most beautiful and desirable woman in the world. She felt as if a chunk of her soul had been ripped away, and she wasn't sure how she would ever feel whole again.

"Not a word," she said.

"He'll call."

"If he was going to, he would have done it by now." It's not as if she hadn't expected this. She knew that when the truth came out, it was going to end. She just hadn't expected it to hurt this much.

"You're probably right," Mary said in that deadpan tone of hers. "I'm sure he's completely forgotten you by now."

Jane shook her head. "I really hate you sometimes."

"Don't tell me you're still mad at him."

"No." Mostly just heartbroken. Because after obsessing over it the entire weekend, she couldn't honestly say that his lie was really any worse than hers. Yes, she had been doing her job, but if she had done it properly, she never would have slept with him. She would have drawn the line. She was just as guilty as he was.

But if he wanted to try to make it work, wouldn't he have called by now?

Maybe the sad truth was that when he had time away from her to think about it, he decided that he didn't love her as much as he thought he did. Maybe she had just been a novelty. Because she may as well face it, men like him didn't love women like her. Only in fairy tales.

"You want to go out and get a drink?" Mary asked. "Or ten?"

Jane smiled. "Maybe some other time."

"If you need to talk, just call. I don't care if it's 3:00 a.m."

"Thanks, Mary."

After another hour, Jane packed up her things and walked out to her car. She considered stopping to pick up dinner, but she wasn't hungry. She hadn't been for days. She drove straight home instead, grabbing her mail and sorting through it as she walked up the stairs. Mostly junk, and a few bills, the usual—

"I was afraid you weren't coming home."

She squeaked with surprise at the unexpected voice and dropped her mail all over the hallway floor.

Next to her door sat Jordan, on the floor, waiting for her.

Her heart instantly jumped up into her throat. He wore jeans and cowboy boots and his black leather jacket.

He pushed himself up to his feet. Then he looked down at the mess she'd made. "Aren't you going to pick that up?"

She crouched down and quickly gathered her mail. Then walked cautiously to her door and pulled out her keys. This didn't necessarily mean anything. Maybe he was just here to return her toothbrush, or to pick up the tie he'd lost under her bed last week.

"Can we talk?" he asked, and maybe it was her imagination, but he seemed nervous. She didn't think he got nervous about anything.

She opened her door and gestured him inside. She closed the door behind them and took off her coat. Normally he wouldn't hesitate to make himself comfortable, but this time he just stood there. She couldn't decide if that was a good or a bad thing.

"You can take off your coat," she said.

He shrugged out of it and hung it on the coat tree beside

hers. He wore an emerald-green shirt that brought out the color in his eyes. He looked so good she wanted to cry. And she wanted so badly to throw her arms around him. She had to force herself to remain rooted to that spot.

"Jane, I screwed up," he said. "I am so sorry for lying to you. And I don't care that you ratted me out. I deserved it. And the only reason I didn't want to tell you that I knew who you were is that I was so afraid of losing you. I just... I can't live without you and I'll do anything—"

Before she even knew what happened her arms were around him and she was holding him, and he was holding her, and she had never felt anything so wonderful in her life. She buried her face in the crook of his neck. "You're forgiven."

He was quiet for a second, then he said, "That was a lot easier than I thought it would be. I really expected to have to grovel."

She laughed and hugged him harder. "Honestly, you had me the second I saw you sitting outside my door. I missed you so much. I *love* you so much."

He caught her face in his hands and kissed her. "Not half as much as I love you. Whether you like it or not, you are stuck with me."

She was so completely okay with that.

"But if this is going to work," he said, "we're going to have to make some changes."

"Changes?"

"Well, first, your car."

"My car?"

"It doesn't suit you."

"It was a gift."

"*Six* years ago. I think you've pushed this polite thing a little too far."

He was probably right.

"We're both going to take Friday off to shop for a new one. And this apartment…" He shook his head. "Either decorate it and get some furniture, or give it up."

"And go where?" Another apartment that she wouldn't furnish or decorate?

"Move in with me. You're there most of the time anyway."

He had a point. She basically only came home to change her clothes and do her laundry. But that was a pretty huge step. "You're sure you want that?"

"Do you think I'm the type of guy to ask a woman to move in with me on a whim? I mean, considering you're the only woman that I ever have asked."

She smiled. "I guess not."

"And the final, most important thing, I want us to be a *real* couple. I want to go on dates—in public. I want to show you off to my friends. And I don't care how obnoxious or overbearing they are, I want to be a part of your family. And I want you to be a part of mine. And if your bosses at Edwin Associates don't like that they can—"

"I quit."

"You did?"

She nodded. "Friday right after I left Western Oil. I'm back at the family practice."

"Is that what you really want?"

"I think so. I definitely want to be practicing law. If not with my family, then at some other firm. But for now I think this is where I need to be."

"I don't know if you heard, but they announced the new CEO."

She held her breath. "And?"

"Emilio Suarez."

"Oh Jordan, I'm so sorry."

"You know, I was so convinced I was in, you would think I'd be really upset, but honestly, I'm okay with it. Emilio is a good guy, and he worked really hard for it. Yeah, I wanted to be CEO, but I'm happy with what I'm doing right now."

"By the way, I didn't get to tell you how amazing it was, what you did for Peter Burke."

"And it almost cost me my job. He was responsible for the explosion."

She touched his cheek. "I heard. I'm sorry he let you down. You deserve better."

He smiled and kissed her softly. "What I deserve, what I *need*, I've got right here."

She hugged him, wondering if this was really real, if maybe she was dreaming.

"Now that we're officially together, you know what this means."

"What?"

He grinned down at her. "I can be your date for the reunion."

She laughed. "Are we back to that again?"

"Come on, I *really* want to go. I even got you something special to wear."

"Like a dress?"

"Nope. Even better. It's in my coat pocket."

What could he have possibly gotten her that would fit in his coat pocket? She reached in and felt something small and hard, and as she wrapped her hand around it she realized it was a ring box. He got her a ring? The question was, what kind of ring?

She pulled it out and looked at it. It was white with the name of a local jeweler in gold on the top, the kind of jeweler only men like Jordan could afford.

This is not what it looked like. As much as she wanted

it to be, it wasn't even possible. It was just too soon, especially for someone like him. Yes, he wanted her to move in with him, but that was a far cry from a marriage proposal. They would probably have to live together for years before he was ready for that kind of commitment. It was probably just a friendship ring. Or maybe even earrings in a very small box.

"Aren't you going to open it?"

She turned to him, gasping when she realized he was down on one knee. "Jordan?"

He grinned. "Open it."

This could not be happening. She opened it with trembling hands, and inside was the most beautiful and the *biggest* diamond engagement ring she had ever laid eyes on. "Oh my God."

"I know it's fast," he said. "But I also know that you're it for me. I think I knew it that first day when you tripped and dumped coffee all over me."

She smiled.

"I love you, Jane, and that isn't ever going to change."

She didn't need years, or even months to know that he was it for her, too. They were supposed to be together. She didn't even know how she knew it. She just knew.

"So ask me," she said.

He gazed up at her with one of those adorable grins. The kind that made her knees go weak. "Jane Monroe, would you marry me?"

"Yes," she said. "Absolutely."

With the promise of everything she could ever want from a husband shining bright in his eyes, he took the box from her, plucked the ring from its satin bed and slipped it on her finger.

* * * * *

COMING NEXT MONTH
Available October 11, 2011

#2113 READY FOR KING'S SEDUCTION
Maureen Child
Kings of California

#2114 MILLIONAIRE PLAYBOY, MAVERICK HEIRESS
Robyn Grady
Texas Cattleman's Club: The Showdown

#2115 BILLIONAIRE'S JET SET BABIES
Catherine Mann
Billionaires and Babies

#2116 A WIN-WIN PROPOSITION
Cat Schield

#2117 THE PREGNANCY CONTRACT
Yvonne Lindsay

#2118 RETURN OF THE SECRET HEIR
Rachel Bailey

You can find more information on upcoming
Harlequin® titles, free excerpts and more at
www.HarlequinInsideRomance.com.

REQUEST YOUR FREE BOOKS!
2 FREE NOVELS PLUS 2 FREE GIFTS!

Harlequin®

Desire

ALWAYS POWERFUL, PASSIONATE AND PROVOCATIVE

YES! Please send me 2 FREE Harlequin Desire® novels and my 2 FREE gifts (gifts are worth about $10). After receiving them, if I don't wish to receive any more books, I can return the shipping statement marked "cancel." If I don't cancel, I will receive 6 brand-new novels every month and be billed just $4.30 per book in the U.S. or $4.99 per book in Canada. That's a saving of at least 14% off the cover price! It's quite a bargain! Shipping and handling is just 50¢ per book in the U.S. and 75¢ per book in Canada.* I understand that accepting the 2 free books and gifts places me under no obligation to buy anything. I can always return a shipment and cancel at any time. Even if I never buy another book, the two free books and gifts are mine to keep forever.

225/326 HDN FEF3

Name _____ (PLEASE PRINT)

Address _____ Apt. #

City _____ State/Prov. _____ Zip/Postal Code

Signature (if under 18, a parent or guardian must sign)

Mail to the **Reader Service:**
IN U.S.A.: P.O. Box 1867, Buffalo, NY 14240-1867
IN CANADA: P.O. Box 609, Fort Erie, Ontario L2A 5X3

Not valid for current subscribers to Harlequin Desire books.

Want to try two free books from another line?
Call 1-800-873-8635 or visit www.ReaderService.com.

* Terms and prices subject to change without notice. Prices do not include applicable taxes. Sales tax applicable in N.Y. Canadian residents will be charged applicable taxes. Offer not valid in Quebec. This offer is limited to one order per household. All orders subject to credit approval. Credit or debit balances in a customer's account(s) may be offset by any other outstanding balance owed by or to the customer. Please allow 4 to 6 weeks for delivery. Offer available while quantities last.

Your Privacy—The Reader Service is committed to protecting your privacy. Our Privacy Policy is available online at www.ReaderService.com or upon request from the Reader Service.

We make a portion of our mailing list available to reputable third parties that offer products we believe may interest you. If you prefer that we not exchange your name with third parties, or if you wish to clarify or modify your communication preferences, please visit us at www.ReaderService.com/consumerschoice or write to us at Reader Service Preference Service, P.O. Box 9062, Buffalo, NY 14269. Include your complete name and address.

HDES11B

*Harlequin Romantic Suspense presents the latest book
in the scorching new* KELLEY LEGACY *miniseries
from best-loved veteran series author Carla Cassidy*

*Scandal is the name of the game as the Kelley family fights
to preserve their legacy, their hearts...and their lives.*

Read on for an excerpt from the fourth title
RANCHER UNDER COVER

*Available October 2011
from Harlequin Romantic Suspense*

"**W**ould you like a drink?" Caitlin asked as she walked to the minibar in the corner of the room. She felt as if she needed to chug a beer or two for courage.

"No, thanks. I'm not much of a drinking man," he replied.

She raised an eyebrow and looked at him curiously as she poured herself a glass of wine. "A ranch hand who doesn't enjoy a drink? I think maybe that's a first."

He smiled easily. "There was a six-month period in my life when I drank too much. I pulled myself out of the bottom of a bottle a little over seven years ago and I've never looked back."

"That's admirable, to know you have a problem and then fix it."

Those broad shoulders of his moved up and down in an easy shrug. "I don't know how admirable it was, all I knew at the time was that I had a choice to make between living and dying and I decided living was definitely more appealing."

She wanted to ask him what had happened preceding that six-month period that had plunged him into the bottom of the bottle, but she didn't want to know too much about him. Personal information might produce a false sense of intimacy that she didn't need, didn't want in her life.

"Please, sit down," she said, and gestured him to the table. She had never felt so on edge, so awkward in her life.

"After you," he replied.

She was aware of his gaze intensely focused on her as she rounded the table and sat in the chair, and she wanted to tell him to stop looking at her as if she were a delectable dessert he intended to savor later.

Watch Caitlin and Rhett's sensual saga unfold amidst
the shocking, ripped-from-the-headlines drama
of the Kelley Legacy miniseries in

RANCHER UNDER COVER

Available October 2011
only from Harlequin Romantic Suspense,
wherever books are sold.